BEST SELLER

Cover design and illustrations: Karla Jarvinen
Back cover photograph: Nadia Lee Cohen
Production and typesetting: Dominik Pollin

First IDEA hardcover edition June 2022.
10 9 8 7 6 5 4 3 2 1

ISBN: 978-1-7395918-0-9

Printed and bound by CPI Group (UK) Ltd, Croydon, CR0 4YY

JUNE NEWTON

BEST SELLER

Her own true story by David Owen

The hour passed her by. ~~Does that sentence even make sense?~~ ~~First lines of books are important!~~ Over two teenage summers, June had sat on this exact same bench, huddled up with her best friend Becky. Together they would split half a pack of ten cigarettes (two each and one to share) and talk about music and films and the lives they were going to lead. They told each other the same jokes about the same people, disguised by ever more obtuse nicknames of which only they would know the origins, if they hadn't themselves forgotten them. This would be the routine, every night, from seven till whenever. Eventually, they would walk back to their family homes on adjacent sides of the park, sucking hard on Extra Strong Mints to extinguish their smoky breath.

It really was a short walk, June now observed, sitting up straight to see over the rise of the cricket pitch. She'd been brought up on the estate directly across from the bench, behind where the swings used to be. Her junior school backed onto the lower side, where the swings were now. It was all very local. Everything that happened or, for the most part, didn't happen, didn't happen here. June took it all in. Then her gaze lowered and fixed on the spot where – and don't be too alarmed when you read this, as it is not as shocking as it sounds – she was shot. It does still sound shocking! But really it was not. There aren't many degrees of being shot, you are either shot or not, but please understand that June was more not than shot.

It was a Friday afternoon after school and eight-year-old June was playing rounders with the Brownies. She was ready to take a swing and, for once, she made a good connection with the ball. Surprised for a second by her own success, June paused before the shouts of her teammates reminded her you were supposed to run. And then she ran fast around the first base and second and... was felled. She dropped to the ground, crying out in shock, horror and a little pain. Blood was running from her knee. She had been shot!

On this mid-May afternoon, some four decades later, June stared longer and harder at the spot where it had occurred, just twenty yards in front of the bench. She was vague about what had happened next – always had been. She was too young, she now supposed, to have built a proper narrative out of such a random and improbable event. Police and parents must have been called because both arrived. She was taken to A&E, she was sure of that. As it was, the pellet had only grazed the knee; they hadn't needed a surgeon to slowly, delicately extract it with steady-hand tweezers and drop it into a metal dish with a tinny 'dink' – not the way June would imagine it now, some forty years later and having watched at least a hundred hours of Nordic noirs on Netflix. No, she just got a butterfly stitch and a plaster on her knee. That evening in 1979, the police had come to the house and told her mum and dad that she had been hit by an air rifle pellet. The teenage son of a family living on the side of the park had set up a shooting range in the garden. The boy claimed he had missed the target and accidentally hit their daughter. Yeah, right, June thought again now; a likely story, as her mum had said at the time. She closed her eyes and sat quite still, and still found no more clarity. She didn't even remember herself when she was eight. The shooting was just a hazy, unreliable memory and not one she even recalled very often... she may not even have told her own sons...

"Hey. Helloooo."

"Oh," June said, opening her eyes, surprised. "Sorry."

Becky was sat with her, perched up on the arm of the bench in a donkey jacket, holding out a half a lit cigarette in the fingertips protruding from her fingerless gloves. June hadn't known she was there.

"Are you alright?" Becky asked.

No, not really, June thought. She didn't take the cigarette. She didn't smoke anymore. "I just lose myself sometimes," she said.

Becky nodded. "Lost in a place you never left."

Oh that's good, June thought. She wished she'd said that.

Becky read her mind. "You give me all the best lines," she said.

June hadn't seen Becky for thirty years. It seemed to her a strange thing for Becky to say.

"One for the book," Becky added.

"The book?"

"Your book."

"Oh, right," June said. She had no idea what her friend was talking about but she went along with it just the same: "Yeah, yeah. If I wrote a book it would be a best seller." June smiled.

"It would," Becky agreed, "and that's what you should call it. 'Best Seller'."

Damn, that's good too, June thought. "I'm not giving you that one," she said.

"It's yours," Becky said, with a smile. She shuffled herself down from the arm and sat in close beside June. "It's all yours," Becky said. "It's so funny that you don't know."

JUNE NEWTON

BEST SELLER

This book is dedicated to the World's Best Dad.

Introduction

This will have to be an introduction to me, I think. It can't be an introduction to the book, for the simple reason that I haven't written it yet. It is also an introduction that you do actually have to read. I know most people jump over these pages to the first chapter. I do it myself. But please do read this introduction, even if you never read another one for the rest of your life!

Also note that I began writing this book in the third person. 'June sat on the bench... June was more not than shot...' That approach has been jettisoned already, sorry. It wasn't very 'me'. It made June/me seem a little too fictional. I am really quite real and accepting this as fact is, I think, kind of crucial. Not so much fun, perhaps, but fundamental to my sanity. It's an important distinction to make. Just so you understand, there really is no difference between June, the character in the book you are reading, and June (being me) who is writing it.

So, hello, whoever you are and whenever you are. You can think of this book as a message in a bottle, written by me in the hope that one day someone will read it and come to my rescue. Actually, no, forget that – it's a bad analogy. You can't write 'Rescue Me' in a bottle now – 'Recycle Me', it would have to be. Besides, many more words than just two will be required to secure my release. I'll lay my cards on the table: I'm aiming to write something with just about as many lines, paragraphs and pages as a very popular paperback book. The kind you would find in a bookshop... at an airport... preferably.

Why am I in need of rescue? The best way to explain it would be to say that my brain is in the wrong place. It is in my head, of course, but my head is on my body and my body is, just to be quite clear about this, definitely not in the right place. Where it is, is here: the small city on the south coast of England where I have always lived and worked and was, in fact, born. I'm not going to name it. It could be any one of ten towns that share a lack of features between them. And the problem with my brain being here is that I have too many thoughts and ideas for this town. Not one too many, either; a lot too many. Far more than are required of a forty-nine-year-old Ladies' Fashions department store manager, that's for sure. What's more, these thoughts are distinctly under-appreciated on a local level. And local is the level, like in a computer game I don't know how to play, that I cannot ever seem to get beyond.

The truth is that I have always had this sense of... I don't know quite how to describe it... being misplaced. Like whatever greater power there is up there was distracted when positioning me. There must have been a knock at the door or a phone call and they will have put me down to deal with it and then forgotten to move me to wherever I was supposed to be. I don't actually believe in higher or greater powers, I am just saying it is *like* that. Unfortunately in recent years my sense of misplacement has become more and more acute. I am often lost in thought. I find myself in conversation with people who don't exist (well, they do exist, just not in my life; I don't know them, not yet anyway). I would say that I am 'losing it' but for the fact that I am not entirely sure I ever 'had it'.

From the outside it all looks normal. From the inside it all looks far too normal as well, that's the problem. I have a family. I have two sons, the second of whom will leave home this year for university. The first has already been and gone – he stayed in Newcastle and lives there now. I am married to my second husband. It is beginning to look like there won't be a third. Ha! I just thought that and wrote it straight down. I don't know what it says about me and marriages, but I like the way it reads so it can stay. Writing is fun. I only hope reading this is equally amusing.

To be a little more specific about my entrapment: just now, while I am writing this, my younger son, the one that hasn't quite gone to university yet, looked up from the BBC News homepage and told me that the new work-from-home trend was bad news for burglars. I said: "Why's that, because they keep robbing themselves?" He didn't laugh. But I still think it's funny. And what can you do with a joke like that, without anyone to tell it to that might actually get it? And just yesterday, by way of further example, there was a half-price lingerie sale in our store. Peggy, who has worked in that department for twenty-seven years, held up a large bra which had lost its label and asked what cup size I thought it was. "I'm not sure about cups," I said, "but you know those bowls the French use for hot chocolate?" Again, that's at least a little bit funny, right? Of course I'd forgotten that Peggy had never been to France. Peggy has never even been to London. She went to Guildford for the day once and, a fortnight later, was still showing me the photos. She is a character. Peggy in lingerie is what I like to call her. As in, "Have you seen Peggy in lingerie?" Anyway, Peggy in lingerie also has a husband, Len, who said he would rather not get a greenhouse – because of the gasses! That is hilarious. That's my favourite Peggy story. But enough about her. This book is not about Peg or her husband.

Anyway, this year, when even less than zero is going on, is also the time in my life so far when I have found myself with the most time to think about how much of a waste of time my life has been. What a long sentence that was! A little harsh on my existence too but, honestly, the things that actually happen to me... well, we are talking about events of a magnitude only particle physicists could detect. The fact is that I am living in a provincial, proverbial hell. A hell where it quite often rains and doesn't get nearly hot enough for my liking.

I have lived here too long. That's the problem. And, with no prospect of moving, it begins to feel like I have just lived too long – and that's not good. That's depressive thinking. I can't have that. This book will be my attempt to write my way out of this paper bag of a life. I appreciate that this is a mixed metaphor. I am leaving it in to demonstrate that I do know what they are, thank you very much. I am sure there will be plenty more to come.

One of these days (quite soon, I imagine) it will be possible to walk right into a movie or television show – like actually inside it. When that does happen, I am quite confident there will be people there that 'get me' immediately: Danny (Adam Sandler) in *The Meyerowitz Stories*; Maggie and/or Chris from *Northern Exposure*; Elaine Benes from *Seinfeld*, naturally. The psychiatrist in *The Sopranos* I could talk to. We could definitely be friends, but then I suppose everyone would say that: she has such a nice face. These are all characters, of course. I am aware that they are fictional. But my hope is that they are at least based on real people. You know, how someone like Agent Cooper, with his quirks and his insights and hunches, might really exist. David Lynch is probably just like that, isn't he? I could have coffee and donuts with him. Peter Falk, I suspect, was basically Columbo. One and the same. But now he is dead. Ten years ago now :(

JUNE NEWTON

Preface

People don't read prefaces either do they? Well, if I am writing a book, I am writing a preface. And here you are reading it!

You know how, when you grow up, people stop asking you what you want to be when you grow up? I think that's sad. It's a shame, don't you think? Certainly no one ever asks me. The fact that I don't really know has nothing to do with it. I'd make something up if they asked! I'd be a spy. That would do it. A really good spy that follows people by walking ahead of them. They do that, the best ones – or so I read. Now, if someone is following me, unlucky! I am following them! Better yet, I could be an assassin. I am so anonymous, no one would ever suspect me. Of course that's also the problem: because I am so anonymous, no one will think to ask me.

If you are a master criminal or a bashful billionaire benefactor, anonymity is great. I am neither and it sucks. I can give you two examples of my hidden-in-plain-sightedness right now. One, I pick up litter. I always have done. If someone drops something, I pick it up. I don't ask for thanks. If you watched any CCTV footage of any day on the high street you would see me. The problem is that they use these cameras to catch criminals and that's why they don't catch me. That's why I will never make the pages of the local paper. All they ever report on is anti-social behaviour – and

I wish it was hermits refusing dinner invitations (that's a proper joke, right there). I could be a CCTV star but, no, it is always the kid who rides a scooter through the window of Ernest Jones that gets all the thumbs up on YouTube.

Second example of my anonymity, and this happened today: an older man, in his late sixties, walked past me. He glanced up at me and straight back down to the pavement in front of him and carried on by. And I thought: What? Not even a second look? I looked back as he passed and he didn't even check back to see my bum. I was wearing a skirt too. Admittedly, I don't have the looks to stop traffic, but pedestrians? Surely I can give them pause for thought.

Novelists create characters that become real for some people. Sherlock Holmes, James Bond and George Smiley all have addresses in London. I am sure many people think they actually existed. And yet, in comparison to their vivid reality, I am virtually non-existent. And I am real! That is why I need to write this book. To create myself. To write myself into existence (and an address in London would be nice too). I just need to stay positive. I don't want this to be a sad book. I don't read sad books. Not after *Watership Down*. I know there is pain and suffering in the world. I can read that on people's faces.

I imagine this book as very delicately poised between poignant and heartwarming. By way of example, my grandmother, on my mother's side, had two angelfish that she called Hopes and Dreams. Even when we were on the phone to her as teenagers, we would ask how her Hopes and Dreams were doing. She'd always say, "Alive and well." We knew they weren't the same fish from when we were really small. Now if I had two fish that is what I would call them – Alive and Well. That's the tone I want to set. This book will be full of humour and insight and ideas and warmth, and I know just the person to write it – June Newton, AKA me.

I'm going to start by writing up a few thoughts that came to me recently, after I decided to start writing. That was last Friday. It looks like I have had one or two good ones every day since. You can read them first. Then, when I am through writing them up, I'll go back in my memory and retrieve some more. I'll add those older thoughts to the new ones I will be having while I am doing that and, in just few weeks, we should soon have something close to a book.

See how I have started using 'we' already. And *we* have only just met!

JUNE NEWTON

My thoughts of the last three days, most recent first.

Age is just a number. So said Joan Collins. This may be true. But it is also true that some numbers are easier on the eye than others. 19, 20, 21–29 are all very pretty numbers. 49, 50, 51 – less so.

Money launderers are the unsung heroes of the acting profession. Running these businesses that look just like real businesses. Staying in character for eight-hour shifts, sometimes even as launderers, which must be doubly ironic.

When you are young, you can discover things backwards. Like Joni Mitchell, say. You hear one song and then go back and listen to all the albums before it. When you get to a certain age, you have caught up. You have to wait for them to make a new album or write the next book. And then you feel, or at least I do, that this is weird: I am living at the same time as David Hockney and waiting for him to finish a painting.

You do things in places you think you'll be leaving. That's one thing about living in the same town your whole life. I might have friends who would come back to this area as adults and point out a spot where they had their first kiss or, you know, other less innocent things. Meanwhile, I am driving to work every day past bus stops and car parks, thinking, Jesus, do you have to remind me?

If there is one thing I would like to be, it would be a cancer survivor. If I am going to get it, I want to beat it. Then when people see me, they will say to each other: "Oh look, there's June. She beat cancer." It would lend me character, I think.

What if you visited a friend's house and found something in their toilet cistern? What could you do? I mean if they had a gun or a thousand pounds sealed up in a plastic bag. Would you anonymously tip off the police? Even that could unravel to the terrible reveal that you had looked. Everyone peeks in their friends' medicine cabinets, right? That's a given. But lifting the lid for a quick check in the cistern? That is very, very socially unacceptable.

To my mind, any one of these thoughts could have been the start of a conversation going on long into the night. Should have been. But they weren't. That's not what happens. Not for me. What I get is... well, here are a few of the most common responses. I have repeated the ones that get said the most frequently:

Huh?

Is that a joke?

Why would you say that?

June did anyone tell you you are weird?

June did anyone tell you you are weird?

June did anyone tell you you are weird?

June did anyone tell you you are weird?

You're strange.

You're strange.

You're strange.

What?

What is wrong with you?

Don't you have any normal thoughts?

Life doesn't have to be like that. Just this evening, I drove home and parked the car in the garage. Before I turned the engine off, I watched the orange light of my indicator flash on and off against the chest freezer we have pushed up against the back wall. I had noticed, when sitting in traffic, that the indicators on different models of cars blinked at different speeds. I had looked to see if there was any correlation between the faster-flashing indicators and the faster, flashier cars but no, sadly, that was not the case. Parked up in my garage, I was taking note of the calm, measured blink of my Hyundai's lights and...

"It worries me a little, I have to say, this toilet cistern business."

It was Joel or Ethan Coen. I'd given one or the other of them a lift home a couple of times before but was still not quite sure which one was which.

"Well," I said. "I was thinking about bathroom cabinets at friends' houses and – do you look in them? The cabinets, I mean."

"Do I ever not?" Joel or Ethan said. "It's expected, right? I expect it of my guests too. I leave just the right amount of embarrassing ointments and medicines in there to make it look real. But I hide anything seriously disturbing."

"What about birth control?"

"Oh yeah. You have to make sure the... what do you call them? Condoms? You have to make sure they are in date. I replace them regularly. And I always open the pack and throw one away. You know, to appear..."

"Like you're not past your sell-by date?" I said.

"Right!" replied Joel or Ethan. "Like I'm in date!"

"But the things you hide, do you ever seal them in a plastic bag and stuff them in the toilet cistern?" I asked.

"No! Why? Do you?"

"No because what if someone looked in there? It would be worse. Like you were truly ashamed."

"It would totally freak me out," Joel or Ethan said. "The only thing you should find in the tank is a gun. Even drugs or money would be a disappointment."

"So do you ever look in them?" I asked.

"No! You can't. It breaks the movie code. Characters hide guns in the cistern and then come back some time later – even years later – and, you know, that's how they shoot their way out of the mob restaurant meeting, even though they were patted down on the way in. If people started checking toilet cisterns wherever they went, that would be the the end of that trope."

"Oh," I said.

"You look in a friend's toilet tank and you would have Martin Scorsese to answer to!"

I turned the engine off. "You know I am going to keep looking in them, don't you?"

"Sure I do. I trust that you will. And I hope that you find something. I really do."

"Thank you," I said.

"Thing is, though," Joel or Ethan said, thinking out loud, "if you did find a gun, who could you tell?"

"That was exactly my point!" I said.

"It's a problem for the police," Joel or Ethan said.

"But the real problem for the police would be..." I interjected.

"... is how can they trust a woman who looks in people's toilet cisterns?" Joel or Ethan closed out the thought.

Today (being Monday 31st May)

Oh dear! The diary format. Don't hate me but I couldn't honestly think of a better way to approach the book. Diaries have been best sellers, haven't they? Samuel Pepys was a little pre-Amazon but he'd have been trending, surely. Adrian Mole, Bridget Jones – both fictional – but ever so popular. Anne Frank is a thought I shouldn't even be having – but too late now.

I am going to use the date format with regular entries but more as a way of recording my thoughts. Please do not think of it as a diary. You would not want to read a blow-by-blow account of my life; really, nothing could be more dull. Besides, I don't like them. And seeing as I commonly misspell 'diary' as 'dairy', I shall say this about dairies: I am lactose intolerant!

Also, by way of full disclosure, I did actually start writing a journal when I was sixteen and was quite excited about it until I walked into my bedroom and found my mother reading it. "I'm so sorry," she said, properly embarrassed, herself. "I really have only read half of one page." "Phew," is what I thought, "that was close." That was before she said: "But I think we should talk about you giving boys blowjobs in the park." You can laugh. It was beyond embarrassing. And she used the plural – twice: 'boys' and 'blowjobs'. Even if this had occurred on more than one occasion (it may have done), I certainly hadn't written about it. I'd only been keeping the diary for a week! So now you know why I do not keep a diary. These dates are just dates, OK?!

There is some actual news for today's entry, however. A

curious crime spree is developing in our store. Someone has been unscrewing the hands off the mannequins and stealing them. "It's the perfect crime," I said to Peggy this morning. "No fingerprints." Blank look from Peg, of course, but I am collecting witticisms for this book now and don't care a jot if she doesn't get them. Of course if the thief takes it further (up the arm) we will end up with a Venus de Milo situation. That image made me think that if I was the manager of a seriously trendy London boutique (as if!), I'd have Greco-Roman statues as the mannequins. I mean, that would be cool, wouldn't it?

Tuesday 1st June

It is not my birthday. Not any day this month. Be given a month name, like April, May or June, and, when that month rolls around, someone will surely ask. It would make sense, but that's not the way it always works. Sometimes people will calculate nine months from now and guess at March – that's if they are smart enough to count in base 12. That would also make sense, but it's not the way it works with me. Born in December and given the name June for the very agreeable reason that my parents both liked it. Sunshine in winter, that's me.

Once you pass the twenty, the ninth year is always going to be a struggle: twenty-nine was agony, thirty-nine was worse. It's the same for everyone, I am sure. If the whole world fell into a hundred-year sleep and then woke up, do you think anything would change? Would we still be clinging onto the decades? 'Oh, she's been saying she's 129 for as long as I've known her.'

For me, forty-nine is an age I can live with. For a long time.

Saturday 5th June

I left work late tonight, after putting all the shoes that customers had tried on back in their boxes, and stacking all the boxes the right way round in the stockroom, so you can see the sizes. You can see how my life story would be such a rollercoaster read, can't you? There are junior floor staff who should be doing this but on a Saturday, well, the lure of the pub and club is just too great. One of the juniors actually said it was above his pay grade! I don't know what HBO series he got this gem from. The reality is that, on a retail sales manager's salary, in this economic climate, even getting out of bed in the morning is above my pay grade.

I have come home to find that the local corner shop has been shut down for changing the dates on yoghurts with a biro! We were all living with this as a known fact for so many years and no one really ever complained. The owner also used to slip new card packaging on out-of-date ready-meals. It's not come out yet whether they discovered that too.

Sunday 6th June

The bodies of two headless birds were discovered on our living room floor. This is not a local mafia thing: this is our cat's contribution to a Sunday morning. My husband saw them first. He coaches kids' athletics and was up early. He shouted up the stairs: "There's two headless birds down here but I've got to get going." Lovely. Later in the day I went for a walk to the seafront and bumped into one of his friends who'd been at the track. He asked if I had forgiven my husband yet. It seems that (I'm not using names, so I will just say 'my husband' again) my husband had been up for a full hour with the dead birds and just didn't fancy dealing with them. I'm not angry. I quite like these insights into how real and flawed (just like me) the people I know and am closest to actually are. Arriving home, I saw my neighbour and she said most people think cats are trying to please their owners by bringing the birds and mice into the house but she'd read on the internet that, actually, they are trying to teach us how to hunt. I thought: if that is true, what else are they trying to teach us? How frustrating it must be for a cat. We find them sitting in the tumble dryer and post a cute pic on Instagram and they were trying to pass on some hitherto unknown law of thermodynamics.

This is also the same neighbour, Miriam, she is called, who once said that she felt lucky never to have won the lottery! I have given that an exclamation mark. What she meant was, she was so content in her suburban mediocrity that millions in the bank could only spoil it. I thought that was stretching it a bit, to say you felt lucky in not winning something that carries a one-in-forty-five-million chance of success. She might be glad she didn't win the lottery, but hardly *lucky*. That would make her unlucky if she *did* win the jackpot: it's not a national game of Russian Roulette.

Now would be a good time to write a little bit about husbands. The current decapitated-bird-averse one is a non-alcoholic. There I have said it. I'm only partly joking too. He doesn't drink. As far as I am aware, he never has. So he would be described as teetotal, I guess, if he wasn't addicted to non-alcoholic wines and beers. It's been going on for a while and obviously I never minded. Why would I? But now he has started hiding bottles around the house. This morning I was trying to find the plastic tool we use to de-ice the fridge and discovered a bottle of Eisberg Rosé behind the washing machine. This is after I found a four-pack of Heineken 0.0 at the bottom of the laundry basket. It isn't something we talk about. If he was an alcoholic alcoholic I would confront him or support him, but this non-alcoholism is just too weird to mention.

We don't actually talk about much, as it happens, and what we do say to each other rarely needs saying – we just confirm things the other person already knows. I don't know if you have ever tried having a conversation with someone where you only say things that the other person doesn't know? I always wanted to try it. I don't imagine it is very smart thing to do in a marriage. From what I can tell, the vast majority of the world's conversations involve discussions and disputes around things that could quite easily be resolved by looking them up online. You know, like whether the launderette is or isn't open on a Sunday, whether this route or that route was the quickest, how many John Hughes films Molly Ringwald was in. Just look it up! Of course in the future we won't need to Google anything, we will be wired to the internet. But this is also, I have now realised, the fatal flaw in Elon Musk's chip in the brain idea. People would know everything. It would kill conversation completely. You couldn't even ask a question without the chip telling you the answer. You'd find yourself saying: "So do you think I need an umbrella? No don't answer that. Got it." All facts would be off the table for discussion. What would be left to talk about? Feelings, probably. And men famously don't like talking about their feelings. Instead of asking my husband: "Who won the game?" I'd have to say: "Mason Mount scored in the 89th minute. How did that make you feel?" That is not going to work.

My current husband is lying next to me now. As I type this he is snoring. I don't really have designs on a replacement but as I am rereading and correcting this day's entry, I am thinking an ideal next husband for me would be an author who loses his mojo. I would secretly carry on his work, winning major literary prizes in the process. That would be just about the right balance of power for me in a marriage.

Monday 7th June

Peggy had the day off today but came in anyway to show off her new husband. He's not technically 'new'. He is still 'no greenhouse gasses' Len but in February this year he had a heart attack and the doctors put him on a vegan diet. It has transformed him. He has lost weight. His skin is no longer the yellowish grey it was before. He smiles. He doesn't leer at women in the same way. His hair is completely white and he's changed the styling of it now too. He used to be in the merchant navy but retired a year before the heart attack. This is the second time I have met the vegan Len and he really is like a different person. I said exactly that to Peggy and she shot me such a look. Chilling. I actually felt a chill, like a cold key down my back*. She couldn't have, could she? (Switched him, I mean.)

*I had to asterisk this one. Younger readers might be confused but the cold key down the back was a hiccup cure when I was a child. Also the cold key or frozen butter knife against the back of the neck was used to stop a nosebleed. Please note that it is not so much that I am old, as it was that my grandparents were already ancient when they did this to me. And they probably got it from their grandparents. My grandparents' grandparents' grandparents would have been subjects of Charles II. Just to give this some context.

Tuesday 8th June

"Which is your favourite hand?" a customer asked me today.

I had never even thought about it. "If I had a million pounds for every time somebody asked me that," I said, "I'd be a millionaire."

"Mine's the left," she said and wandered off.

The hand question is a tough one. I honestly can't decide! I am looking at them both. Then just one and then just the other. One has a wedding ring. The other has a couple of rings. Other than that they are the same. I am right-handed, so I could favour that one, but these days I am typing a lot and that requires both of them to work together. Even if I picked one, just for the sake of answering, I would feel I was doing the other one a disservice. It's a good thing we were quiet in the store today; I looked at my hands until the lunch break and still no decision.

It was quiet in the afternoon too. Only one notable moment when I told a customer: "You don't need retail therapy. You need a hat." Very Dorothy Parker!

I was working alongside Sandra, who has a retired guide dog. She only covers our department occasionally and for a few hours I get a couple of months' worth of canine updates. Today I said that rather than teaching dogs tricks, wouldn't it be much more impressive if someone taught a dog to perform the same tricks on them? I would watch a YouTube video of a dog owner lying on their back, arms and legs splayed, while the dog tickled their stomach. Or a dog hurling a stick from its mouth for the owner to go fetch. I didn't think it would be so difficult. I asked Sandra if she thought Barney might be capable of learning to make her do the tricks. "He probably could do it," Sandra said, thinking hard. "But I don't know that I could hold out that long for the chocolate treats."

Tomorrow brings a totally unnecessary but very welcome training day in London. Actually, almost London: it's in Mitcham, which is technically Surrey. But even so, anywhere inside the M25 is like a different time zone for me.

Wednesday 9th June

Trains literally and metaphorically transport me. I love them. This morning, double-delight, I found a newspaper with an unfinished crossword. I like to see where they got stuck. A completed crossword is such a disappointment, no one likes a know-it-all! This person – I am guessing a man, but that's probably sexist of me – had this question unanswered.

Obfuscated clue (7)

It wasn't cryptic, but the answer was. I filled it in and put the newspaper down. I was booked on the train after all the commuters had gone to work and there was plenty of real, everyday-life entertainment to enthral me. A woman with a baby was sat diagonally opposite. An older woman, maybe the mother or grandmother was opposite them, knitting. I love women who knit on public transport *and* women who breastfeed on public transport. I thought that if I had another child I would do both. I would start breastfeeding and quickly crochet a screen for our privacy. I wanted to tell them this but if there is anything to start a conversation with, it is not that. Plus the baby started crying and I did wonder if you are allowed to take babies on the quiet carriages of trains. I know you are not supposed to use phones on them and this baby was a lot louder than most callers. As we approached Mitcham Junction, I was imagining two babies on the phone to each other, both of them just screaming down either end.

The training day was, of course, pointless. A new stock control system to make everything quicker and more efficient. Well, yes, I thought, it would be, if you had any sales to put through it. No one I know wants to spend money, certainly not our customers. The objective for them is to wake up on Monday morning and go to bed the following Sunday night having spent nothing. This is what makes working in regional retail so depressing. Occasionally it will be forecast for rain long enough that someone has to buy some boots, or a woman's handbag will actually fall apart and leave her no choice but to buy a new one. All our sales are made under sufferance. Having to buy things makes these people miserable. The truth is that our customers have in-disposable incomes.

I still enjoyed the away-day. Everything is faster. You don't notice it so much when you are there – what I imagine is evidence of the theory of relativity. But when you step back out of the zone, it's like the first steps you take at the end of the travelator at the airport; a clunky stumble as your body adjusts to the hard and fixed reality. I feel the local slow time most at the supermarket checkout. In London they are practically grabbing your groceries out of your basket, pressing the self-service buttons for you, to speed it all through. At home, oh, the agony, the cashier won't even start up the conveyor belt until the person before you has paid, packed up their shopping and driven fully out of the car park. Strangely, it seems that the older people get, the less they complain about these long waits. There will be someone over eighty in the queue and I'm looking at them, thinking: 'I hope you have planned this out. Just how long do you think you have you got?'

Is it possible that people can get so old that they start seeing best-before dates on rice or pasta as some kind of abstract irrelevance? You know, like they read 'Jan 23' with some wishful, wistful beside-the-pointness?

I'm forty-nine and I count all the sunny days.

Thursday 10th June

Back to life. Back to reality. *Sigh* as Charlie Brown would say. There is no funny anecdotal way of telling the story of why I never left town. So I will just lay it out.

I sat my A-levels. I had an offer to read English. I got the grades. But then my mother became sick. It was a debilitating illness but not a quick diagnosis. After six months it was decided she had ME (not 'me' – I was no burden to her, unlike my brother). She had chronic fatigue syndrome, as they call it now. She stopped working. My dad didn't cope very well. My brother was absent without leave again. Truth is that my brother wasn't around when my parents were bringing him up. I deferred my university place for a year. I won't say which university it was, as it only breaks my heart. Mum didn't get better. I got a job (yes, in the same department store I work in now). Mum's health did improve but by then I had already met my first husband. And then I was pregnant. And then married. I needed to be on maternity leave for the money, so I kept my job. When my son was older, I went back to work. We bought a house. We had a second child. Then we divorced. Then I was offered a promotion. I met my second husband. We bought a house. The boys grew up. The elder one went to university. The younger one is just about to follow him in October. That is what happened. That is how it happened. And, all the time, I was meant to leave. I should have been gone.

Now if someone asks me if the book I am writing is autobiographical, I'll say, yes, in part, almost a whole page.

Friday 11th June

Lunch with Tina today. I have known her for years. The first time we met was as strangers in the leisure centre pool. She swam quicker than me but we found ourselves at the same end between laps on more than one occasion. When it comes to swimming, I'm about half and half time spent actually swimming and time wasted, holding on to the edge of the deep end, considering my next move. So ours was synchronised swimming but in a very *'even a watch that has stopped shows the right time twice in a day'* kind of way.

We got chatting about being on our lunch breaks and the men who powered up and down in furious front crawl, and how hot the hot chocolate from the machine in the foyer was (tongue scalding) – you know, as you do. And then we got out – from different ends – but at the same time. We both went to the showers and this time I was quicker than her (although I can't take much pride in that; swimming being an Olympic sport and speed-showering not even a recognised hobby). I was in my underwear when Tina came out of the shower area and we discovered that our lockers were side by side. We must have said something to each other then too; I don't remember. It was as we got dressed that we realised, item by item, that we were really very different people. Same age, more or less, but very different. For my suit trousers, her sparkle-flecked tights and short, stonewashed denim skirt. My pinstripe blouse and her sweatshirt with appliqué unicorns – yes, two! She added hoop earrings so big that, on sight of the first one, I expected her to put her hand through it and wear it as a bangle.

I was still a few steps ahead of her, but when I came back from the hairdryers to say goodbye, she'd scraped her towel-dried hair up into one of those up-do's (Pompey Pineapples they call them in Portsmouth and everywhere else on the South Coast) and was ready to leave. So we walked out together. She lit a cigarette and said she was getting the bus. I offered her a lift if she was going my way and then, somehow, for reasons neither of us could properly explain, we have stayed in touch. And we have met up once every couple of months ever since – again for no particular reason other than it is what we do.

If I try and rationalise it, we met the first time in those certain circumstances and, as those circumstances have not changed, we have continued to meet. We are friends with nothing in common apart from the single binding element of having nothing in common. One day it will be on the BBC News that scientists in the Hadron Collider have found sub-atomic particles that have nothing in common apart from having nothing in common. 'It was the hypothesis of Ladies' Fashions Floor Manager, June Newton (no relation) and now it has been observed and proven to be true.'

This quantum theory is not something I shared with Tina. Usually she will talk and I will listen. That's fine with me. Today, though, she was midway through telling me of her brothers' (and I do mean that apostrophe to be after the 's' – there are two of them) clandestine affairs with the same married woman, and she just stopped and asked me if I was alright. She said I looked different. Like something had happened. Like something had changed. Interesting, I thought. The only thing that had changed was that I had started writing. Could she tell that from the way I was listening and at the same time thinking of the brother's or brothers' punctuation? Should I tell her?

"I'm writing a book," I said.

"Really," she said. "What, like *Fifty Shades of Grey?*"

I have left a line break after that comment. At the time I just mumbled something in reply and we finished our lunch of open sandwiches (they have been the new thing round here for the last twenty-two years). When we were leaving, Tina said, "You should write a self-help book." I took that as a compliment. Although, if this book is helping anyone, it is me.

Friday 18th June

I was the only one with an umbrella today and it rained! This is because last year I got so fed up with the plain wrongness of the BBC weather forecasts that I set my phone app to show the Shetland Islands as my 'home'. I would recommend it to anyone. Never a dull moment, however many are forecast!

To myself, in my head, but sometimes out loud, I use the phrase 'Spoiler Alert' when performing a tricky task. I haven't done any baking in a while but it used to be when I came to add the vanilla flavouring or set the oven timer that I'd say 'Spoiler Alert!' and double-check to make sure I didn't ruin the cake. I said it again today before signing an all-staff leaving card for Beryl in accounts. There is always someone that blotches them or spells their own name wrong. Not me.

Saturday 19th June

Current husband and I went round to Leg and Pen's for dinner. We call them that – Peg and Len. This is an annual invite. For the past two years we had managed to get out of it. Two years back, it was our eldest son's graduation that provided the excuse and last year, quite fortuitously, my husband already had food poisoning! This year I accepted on our behalf. It was promised that Len would be cooking and it would be vegan. That in itself should cut down the chance of serious illness, I thought. Added to that, I had been fascinated by the new Len, ever since Peg flashed me the spine-tingling look.

Inside the Hutchins' house, I was in major sleuth mode. While Len was in the kitchen and Peg was fixing us drinks, I checked out the photos in the lounge. There were Leg and Pen in their wedding photo. This would have been 1980 or thereabouts. I barely recognised the flush-faced Peggy, let alone the tall, dark, handsome Len. More recent photos were decidedly absent. There was no Len after 1980. I thought about our family photographs; we don't display them. We were strictly album-only while the boys were growing up and, after the advent of camera phones, well, they are all floating somewhere in the cloud, on social media or, basically, lost.

The new Len has a pacemaker. I said that all world leaders should be fitted with pacemakers so that their heart rates can be monitored by the United Nations. When numbers climb steeply or fall off a cliff, the world would be on high alert. "Pacemakers for peacemakers," I called it. Len thought this was funny. There was no response from Peggy or my husband. They are used to me by now, I guess. And then, quelle surprise, the new Len turns out to be a good cook. Bombay Burritos with a fresh seasonal salad. Very edible. "We grew the tomatoes ourselves," Len said, nodding out to the garden. I looked out through the French windows and there it was – a greenhouse.

"A greenhouse?" I said, looking to Peggy for a response. She pursed her lips. "No gasses?" I asked.

"Sorry?" said the new Len.

"Peggy said you were worried about the greenhouse gasses."

Peggy jumped in: "I never said that."

"Ha. I get it," said Len. "That's funny. Greenhouse gasses. June you are very funny."

"What's funny?" This was my husband.

"Nothing," said Peg. "Just June being weird... again."

We drove home. No talk about the new Len. My husband was already focused on the next morning's athletics. He went straight up to bed, fast asleep in seconds, no doubt. The night was warm so I opened the back door and took a glass of wine outside.

"OK, run this by me again. You think the new Len is actually a new 'Len'?" Nicolas Cage was sat sprawled in a garden chair.

"If he is the same man, he is not the *same* man," I said.

"So she swapped him out? The old switcheroo?" Nicolas asked.

"I'm exploring that possibility? Is it so unbelievable?"

He gave it some thought. "Eighty percent of all the people in the world are religious. Sixty-five per cent of Americans think aliens exist and one in three American millennials believe the earth is flat."

He had all these figures to hand. I wondered if film actors had lines scripted for their lives off-screen. You know, they work with a good writer on a movie, then on their day off they WhatsApp them for some dialogue to use at the supermarket...

Nicolas hadn't finished with his piece. "The way I see it, all these people are looking in the wrong place – their scope is too big. They want to believe in life after death, in ghosts or parallel universes. They think a huge event like the moon landing was faked or that the holocaust never happened..."

"Yes," I said. "When it is actually the quantum sub-atomic physics that really can't be explained. That's where the awesome stuff is happening."

"Awe and then some."

"That's good! Awe and then some."

"Thanks," Nicolas said.

He wouldn't say thanks if someone else had written it, would he? It was such a good line.

Nicolas sat himself up to press home his point: "What I mean to say is, people look in the wrong place. They can't actually look at quantum particles because they are too small to see and they don't affect people's everyday lives. But the truly inexplicable, impossible stuff – if it does happen – is, by this logic, more likely to be small-scale, barely noticeable things. Like finding a cupboard door is open when you are sure you shut it or..."

"A new Len taking the place of the old Len," I said.

"Exactly. Now what we have to wonder is, does Peg know?"

"You mean...?"

"I mean, I am sure she knows. He's a different man. But maybe she wasn't in on it. One Len goes into hospital and another Len comes out. The new Len is better."

"Better at everything."

"Right. So what does she do? Send him back? Or..."

"Go with the flow."

"And the old Len..." mused Nicolas, "is..."

"Dead," I said.

He nodded in agreement. "Dead, yes. Or living in... what's your equivalent of New Jersey?"

I didn't need to answer that. I just gestured to the suburbia surrounding us.

Sunday 20th June

I have now seen, courtesy of Facebook, that my first husband has taken up medieval battle re-enactment. That is how he is spending his middle age – in the Middle Ages! Every weekend, he is off with his new wife, jousting, eating spit-roasted boar and laughing at jesters, if you can believe that. Goodness. I quite like Yazoo and The Human League but that's as far back as I go. I certainly wouldn't dress up like them. I see from the news that pirates are having a moment too, although I don't think the Somali sea bandits do the whole eyepatch, parrot on the shoulder, wooden leg thing, do they? As for my ex-husband's medievalness, there will surely come a time when one of these battle re-enactments runs up against a modern-day act of terrorism. Like on London Bridge when that guy tackled the terrorist with a spear, but multiplied by the hundreds. I'd pitch it as a film, if I were a film pitcher, that is. The terrorists would ultimately have to be overcome, of course, that's Hollywood, but not before scores of battle re-enactors, first husband included, were slain.

There is not a cat's chance in hell that I would have done that chainmail and chalice stuff with him when we were together. In medieval times I would likely have been burnt at the stake for being a witch. "Do your worst!" I would scream in pain. "I'll only end up with a sainthood."

Saint June – Patron saint of smart-arses.

My first husband and I definitely had our moments, though. We met on New Year's Eve, 1991. We were together for the Millennium with our first child. There was a party. There was karaoke. We sang *Up Where We Belong* from *An Officer And A Gentleman*. Neither of us were good singers so I took the gravel-voiced Joe Cocker part and my husband warbled Jennifer Warnes. It was the best way out of a nerve-racking situation for us both. We weren't such a bad team, looking back on it now. We could improvise. We were ace doubles partners at pool. He was actually very good and could pot pretty much everything. I was completely hopeless. Our great insight was that I was just as likely to miss the easy red, sitting begging over the pocket, as I was to pot the mathematically impossible wonder shot. So I might as well shoot for the moon. He would place his finger on the cushion where I needed to aim and, whack, the balls would scatter and I would quite often pot a reverse-double with a two-ball cannon plant (had to look up this lingo, btw). I loved it. I have memory-ache thinking about it now. That is what it does; my memory aches.

Sunday 27th June

A week has elapsed. It's been lost. Seven days is not by any measure the longest period of time to have gone missing in my life but I had thought that the discipline of writing was helping. I was looking for things to write and making things happen and then, this past week, nothing but ennui.

I've got to stop taking baths – that's part of the problem. It's like bathing in memories. The shower is still 'in the now': it's all about my body and what I have to do today. The bath, well, I soak myself back to 1987 or 1992 or whenever; specific moments, conversations and events that I replay over and over. It's very seductive and I appreciate the re-experiences. The problem is that as I travel back in time, the actual time continues to move forward. I can't stop the clock for a reminisce. I lie in the bath until the water gets cold, and although I may have drifted back to the day before my eighteenth birthday, I still emerge twenty minutes older than when I got in. The wrinkles are from the bath water – but they don't all smooth out.

The older you get, the more of the past there is behind you. Maybe age is a percentage indicator. Now I am 49% past and 51% present and future. By the time I am eighty, sitting in the same chair all day in a nursing home, 80% of all my brain activity will be spent processing memories. Eight out of ten things I do and see I will have seen and done before. I bet it's actually higher than that. I'm not ready for it yet; it is coming on too quick. So far this week I haven't done anything that I haven't done before. There hasn't been anyone I have met that I haven't met before. And it is Sunday again already! I need to start creating new memories, if only to give the old ones a little less space. My teenage years must think they've found a cheat hack in Minecraft. They are running rampant, building mind palaces in all available spaces. New experiences is what I need. To turn off the memory tap.

Monday 28th June

I should be having them and I am not: new experiences, I mean. I need at least one a week. Below is a list of possible activities and my response to the very thought of them.

Threesome – *definitely not.*
Other sex things – *can't even bring myself to write them down.*
Drugs – *yeah, right.*
Smoking – *not a new experience and better off without it.*
Shoplifting – *I work in retail.*
Embezzling – *not enough money in retail.*
Eat real sushi (not Marks and Spencer) – *hmmm, interesting.*
Trip to Japan – *would solve local low-quality sushi problem.*
White water rafting – *massively unappealing.*
Gambling – *not the worst idea on this list.*
St Johns Ambulance – *why would I even think of that?*
Salsa class – *every woman I know already does it.*
Yoga – *really? Do I have to?*

Tattoo – *Lord, no.*
Amateur detective – *watch this space.*
Sleep outside – *in the garden?*
Paintballing – *what is this, 2005?*

Tuesday 29th June

It rained all day today. I swiped through the weather app on my phone and it was raining all day in New York too. Fair enough, I thought, but at least there it is raining *on something*.

A customer told me they needed their 'Raymond Wheel' watch repaired. They meant 'Weill', of course. The watch was a Weill and was not actually vile. I always wondered if foreign brands suffer from having unpronounceable names (for us Brits, anyway). Perhaps this is the real reason for the boom in online sales? There's a balance, isn't there, between chic and exclusive and too-embarrassing-to-say-it-out-loud? Like Loewe (*low eurgh vey*). By way of example, I have never bought either of my two husbands Vilebrequin swimming shorts – although that may be more down to them being £180 a pair, rather than the fact that I can't say the brand name. Vilebrequin patterns are, of course, a little bit vile – but that is all part of the point of them, I think, rather than a clue to the correct pronunciation.

Also today – on much the same subject – I bought my first designer item! Just a small thing, because I can't very well turn up to work one day in a Chanel suit, as if I could anywhere near afford one. Plus I am doing it for me, not everyone else. It has to be something only I will know about. It couldn't be underwear, as that might be misinterpreted by husband as, well, you know, a signal. So I bought a belt online. From Balence-ee-aga. Two hundred and fifty pounds!

Wednesday 30th June

I have author anxiety! I'm now genuinely worried that I don't have enough thoughts. I just flicked through a book I bought but haven't read yet (because I am busy writing), Joan Didion's *Where I Was From*. It isn't a big book but word for word, my God, there is a lot of it! I don't expect to write half as well as Joan Didion did but I would like, at least, to write half as much.

A pocketbook has been purchased during my lunch break. I am writing this in it now. At work! Unofficially, I am working two jobs. I am moonlighting under strip lighting. Already a new starter in stock control has asked me what I am writing down. "Small indiscretions," was my reply. They are my indiscretions, not his, but he is not to know that.

I do worry, though, about this book being 'unfinished' and that I never may never get to the end of writing it. I am not sure I have finished anything in my life other than a box of Celebrations, and that is nothing to be proud about. I have 'ended' a marriage, but that's not the same as 'finished'; he is the father of our boys to start with and still on the scene. The notebook will help me. I am going to complete this. I'm taking myself off to finishing school.

I have just re-read the introduction to this book. Hmmm. I am a better writer already but should I change it? It might lose its charm. Thinking about it, though, how would you know? I'll make you a promise, I won't change it.

My Balenciaga belt arrived! Next-day delivery! I love it. But only as much as I love the packaging. Who knew? The box! The base I am using already for earrings. The top I am using in the study for pens. The felt drawstring bag is perfect for personal things and is in my handbag now. I even kept the tissue paper! And then there is the belt itself. I'm wearing it now – albeit at home. No one has noticed it so no one has mentioned it. How completely perfect. It is mine. And mine alone.

Thursday 1st July

More war reports from the retail apocalypse.

"Look out. Here comes Marge," Sandra said today. That's what we say in the store when we see a customer who is between a medium and a large. They will always think they are 'M' but will be mostly 'arge'. If you are wondering, I would be a 'Smedium' and mostly 'medium'.

'Netflix and chill' is such a valuable phrase – for Netflix, I mean. The company I work for has absolutely no chance of entering the language like that. The best we could hope for would be 'Shop here and look like Maureen Lipman'. No one even steals anything – apart from mannequins' hands and, extraordinarily enough, they have started appearing back on the dummies again! 'It's like they are handing themselves in,' would have been my joke but I didn't bother making it – it's deflating having a crime undone before you can solve it. The only interesting thing that has ever happened around here and now the thief has stolen that from us too.

I do feel something for this store. Same for the high street and the whole pedestrianised shopping precinct. I never knew anything else really; the Coke Float at Beale's, the lemon meringue pie at Dingles, the wishes made when throwing pennies into the goldfish pond by the café at Landports. These were the things I clung to when I was a girl. These were also the things I carried into my adult life. From child to teenager, to a mother with children of her own. Now department stores have shut and the cafés closed. They have all but one of them gone. I have outlived them. I have outstayed their welcome. Sadly it does not feel in any way like I have won.

First full day of Balenciaga belt-wearing at work and no comments. I wonder if I can fully become someone else, incrementally – accessory by accessory.

Friday 2nd July

I had lunch with the new Len today. I really shouldn't have but he came by the store at just the right time for my break. And he is quite charming. Of course I asked about Peg.

"She's away," said Len. "Short break."

"Really?"

"With her friend Sandy. For the weekend."

"An away break? Abroad?"

"No!" Len laughed. "Salisbury!"

"Does Peggy even have a passport?"

"She has one but it only covers Hampshire and Sussex. She's an illegal in Wiltshire."

The new Len is funny. We had our lunch at the one and only vegetarian café in town. He is, I should remind you, a good fifteen years older than me. This is not even remotely a romantic thing. I went for lunch for two reasons: one, as I said, he is amusing. He passed me the salt and his shirt brushed over his lentil shepherd's pie. "Look at me," he said, "wearing my veganism on my sleeve." And two, I was super curious. I wanted to know if the new Len knew he was the new Len. In short, would he confess to the switch? Sadly, the answer was no. He didn't talk much at all about life with Peg before his heart attack. "The past is another country," he said, misquoting *The Go-Between*. I corrected him, but only to show off my literary knowledge. "I saw the film," Len said. "With Peggy?" I tried to ask as innocently as possible. "Now *that* I don't remember," was his reply. Vague... he could be on the cover of *L'Uomo Vague**, this man.

I told Len my best vegan story, which also just happens to be my best story, vegan or otherwise. My uncle's family is vegan and always has been. When my cousin Janet was about eighteen she started dating a man called Hugo Cash (I am not making that name up, by the way). She is now married to him and called Janet Cash. Anyway, about a year after they met they went up to Scotland to meet his parents and brothers and sisters. Janet was a little nervous about being a vegan at a Highland family dinner and more so when she found there were eleven members of the Cash clan around a huge dining table. Whenever Hugo's aged grandmother spoke, she spoke very loudly, as people do when they are either partially deaf or listening to music on headphones (old Mrs Cash would have been in the former group). The food was brought out, including a gigantic roast and, as the family started to help themselves and Janet sat, as yet without food, Grandmother Cash silenced the table by saying, 'No need for you to worry, young Janet. Hugo told us about you. We all know you are a virgin.'

Len laughed. "Oh God," he spluttered.

"I know!" I said. "'Vegan!' Hugo had shouted back, but it was too late."

"That's unbelievable," Len said.

"Yes. Janet was really a very timid girl too. The rest of the family thought it was hilarious. They didn't correct the grandmother and kept going. 'Hugo's mother was a vegan too,' her husband and Hugo's father said, 'until she met me.' 'Have you never been tempted?' one of Hugo's sisters said. 'Not even a little sausage?' said the other."

Len loved it all. I tried to pull the conversation back to his previous life but to no avail.

"Tell me a secret," I asked, at the end of the hour. Quite a blatant attempt, I know.

"The Queen supports Arsenal," said Len.

*David helped me with this one. You haven't met him yet. I was trying to make the joke of Len being on the cover of 'Vague', like 'Vogue', but that's for women. But David knows there is one for men called 'L'Uomo Vogue'. It's Italian, by the way.

Saturday 3rd July

No one I meet at work could be described as eccentric. That is actually my polite way of saying no one I meet at work could be described as interesting. The closest I ever got was about ten years ago, when one of the sales reps at the Christmas party told me he did Tai Chi on the toilet. Just the arms and upper body, as he emptied his bowels. He sat down next to me and showed me. He left the company the next year. Left the area too, I think. I didn't speak to him again after the Christmas party. On his last day we happened to pass each other in the canteen. He looked me and up and down and said, "You should do it."

I would like to be more eccentric myself – externally, I mean.

At least a little more visible. The only people who wear bright colours round here are down holes in the street fixing gas leaks. I was our department's designated fire officer for six months but was off sick on the day of the drill so never even got the chance to style out the hi-vis jacket. All my work clothes have been distinctly lo-vis. In fact everyone I know dresses not to stand out. It's not just normcore, my world, it's anoncore. As senior floor manager I can choose my own clothes but it is still a 'uniform' that I have to wear: a trouser or skirt suit and a blouse. I have worn the same thing for twenty years, and a brown nylon dress for a decade before that. However, now that I have written this – expect change! On Monday I am going to wear something 'hi-vis'. I will report back.

Sunday 4th July

People are still talking about 'Me Time', aren't they? That's the last thing I want. I want some of someone else's time. I want my husband to answer the phone, saying: "Sorry, June can't be disturbed – she's on Zoom with the pipeline activists, editing a script about a miscarriage of justice and auctioning all her awards and wardrobe for the local orphanage. *She's having a bit of Susan Sarandon time.*"

As it was, I had lots of June Newton time today and what did I do with it? I wrote about Branston Pickle. I'm really not joking. Branston has been a constant and important part of my life! I have eaten it since I was a child. Safe to say, I love it. But back in the seventies it was seriously chunky and lumpy. I don't think I read the small print until I was in my teens, but the pickle ingredients were actually a long list of everything I wouldn't eat. The list for me begins with swede. It could end there, to be honest. But it goes on to include more root and unrooted vegetables: the kind you see covered in mud in the farm store: turnip, carrot, onion, cauliflower. The outsize size of these solids in the pickle has led to a lifelong preference for baguettes, rolls or doorstep-cut sandwiches. An inch of bread above and below the chunks was the general equation. As I got older and more independent, that time that educationalists might call puberty or the rubicon (but I think more the age of making my own sandwiches), I would dip the knife deep into the pickle jar and draw it out from the lumps like Arthur's sword. I'd be making lumpless sandwiches for a month but always in the knowledge that one of the days in the weeks ahead, my dad would unscrew the lid of that jar and find... well, I can hardly describe it... the horror of the dry lumps!

But then the story takes the most amazing Saul-into-Paul-on-the-road-to-Damascus twist. Out of the blue (and I forget exactly what year this happened) Branston Small Chunk appeared! I had had never known a brand to make the right decision before. Didn't everyone always moan about changes to recipes or names? No one preferred Choco Krispies to Coco Pops, did they? Kellogg's had to change it back. But here was something so welcome and needed and so aligned with my life story, that it just knocked me out: Small Chunk Branston. I tried, at the time, to explain my enthusiasm to Peggy, who didn't eat pickle and couldn't have cared any less about it. I said: "Imagine there was a company making sun loungers. And the mattresses they designed had rocks and rubble in them. The company's customers struggled to relax in the sun, twisting their bodies to avoid the bricks. This went on for years – 'Like It *And* Lump It' was the company slogan. Then one day a young executive looked at the people contorted in agony and said to his boss: 'I have an idea. What if we made the mattresses smooth? They'd be comfortable.' The boss was shocked: 'What? No lumps at all?' To which the young Richard Branston (I called him that) replied: 'Smaller. We'll make the lumps smaller.' And the new slogan was 'Not Lumpless: Less Lumpy'."

That's probably enough about pickle for now.

I heard a scientist on the radio talking about luck. He's written a book about it. Dr Richard Wiseman, he is called. He conducted an experiment with groups of people who define themselves as lucky or unlucky. They were all given a newspaper that had been prepared with special adverts hidden in it saying they had won a cash prize. The volunteers for the trial weren't told about the ads. They were instead asked to count all the photographs in the newspaper. The results of the experiment clearly showed that the ones who self-identified as lucky discovered the free-money ads on first glance. The self-declared unlucky ones didn't see them at all. Hmm. I totally accept the findings and the science, but what freaked me out was this: the lucky ones know who they are.

That's terrifying. Never mind whether you are male or female, born into riches or poverty, hardworking or lazy: *the lucky ones know who they are*.

"Cheer up, sleepy June," Keanu said. This was his default greeting for me. "You don't think of yourself as lucky?"

"Does it have to be a binary yes or no answer?" I asked.

"Depends what game you're playing," Keanu replied. "If you were just flipping a coin..."

"I think that people who think they are unlucky call tails," I said.

"No. It's cool to call tails. Even though it's fifty/fifty, tails is the left field, left-handed, John McEnroe kind of call. It's like major and minor keys in music. A minor key is for the hopelessly romantic artist. If you call tails and it comes up tails, that's cool. A cool call."

"Like smoking," I said, without really thinking.

"Smoking is cool?" Keanu asked.

"Yes, because you know it is most likely going to kill you. It's a cool call because if you do it and you don't die young... it's a sweet win. The underdog wins."

"So what do you call?" Keanu asked.

"Heads," I said, "and I don't smoke."

"You can't be lucky then," Keanu resolved. "As you said, the lucky ones know who they are."

We stood for a while pondering the probability that he and I were both right. Then he put his hand into his pocket.

"We can flip a coin now," Keanu offered. "One of your British pounds."

"But who is going to call first?" I asked.

"Let's both call at the same time. OK? I'll flip it and we call out at once."

Keanu flipped the coin.

"TAILS!" he called, as I called, "HEADS!"

Keanu put his hand over the coin and, without looking at it, put it back in his pocket. "Let's never know," he said.

I am sure Keanu Reeves keeps the best company. As far as I am concerned, he keeps my company the best. He is so wise.

Monday 5th July

Today I wore my son's three wolves howling at the moon T-shirt to work. Only that is misleading. I wore it to work but not at work. I am so sorry. I don't know why I feel I am letting you down. A fictional me would have worn it all day. But I am not that person. I am the actual real me. I wore it to work with a could-be-beige/could-be-grey skirt-suit and then lost my nerve. I changed, in the car park, into a cream pussy-bow blouse. You have to understand the level of conformity that operates in this area. Honestly, the department store I work in could be campaign HQ for the Normal Party. There are acts of subversion like listening to The Smiths in your car and then there is packing the basement of the Houses of Parliament with gunpowder kegs. My wearing that T-shirt was more in line with the latter example.

Youngest son also has a James Dean T-shirt saying *Too Young To Die* on it. I have no idea where he got it, the internet probably. I am considering making my own response shirt: *Too Old To Live*. But actually *Too Old To Die* would be more accurate. Like I said before, I have problems finishing things. I don't worry about dying. I may never get round to it.

Tuesday 6th July

I haven't named my husbands in this book. They have regular names, in case you were curious. If they were shapes, you would recognise them – like an oval or a pentagon. My sons have regular names too. If they were household appliances they'd be the kind of things you find in every home: a toaster or a kettle perhaps. If I had my time again I might do it differently. A disproportionate number of successful and famous people seem to have irregular names. Elon Musk, for example, and that's the second time he's been mentioned in this book already! The man who presents the Radio 3 breakfast show is called Petroc Trelawny. Uncommon names don't bestow people with uncommon talent but, maybe, they do imbue the bearer of the name with an expectation of greatness that some of them rise up to meet. I am writing all of this with the IKEA catalogue open in front of me. That's what has given me the idea. On the one hand, I am looking at pages of side tables and rugs, and, on the other, I am reading the most creative baby names reference ever printed. Minnen is no more a peculiar name for a boy as it is for an extendable bed. Jonaxel is a great name! Much better suited to my younger son, as it happens, than it is to a modular storage unit. I had actually wanted to call my sons Sony and Casio but my squarely-named first husband said they'd be bullied at school. "For what?" I asked him. "Having cool names?"

Wednesday 7th July

Private account. That's me on Instagram. You never know who is looking otherwise. By all means, follow me down the street in real life. Then I'll decide if I want to drag you inside my house and show you my new kitchen.

Thursday 8th July

Writing this book is taking up more and more of my time. I'm staying up later and then, when I do get to bed, I'm scribbling notes in the dark that I struggle to read in the morning. There's less time now for anything but work and writing, which is also work. The evening meal has gone. I'm not cooking. I'll just have two bowls of cornflakes or a cheese and pickle sandwich. I have been looking for more time-saving efficiencies too. Teeth cleaning is a big one: I spend way too much time on that. I'm not cutting it out completely, you understand, but I am down to a quick brush round and no flossing. It's overhyped, in my opinion. Hygienists are the worst. Zealous preachy leaflet bashers. Always, quite literally, in your face. They're not even proper dentists and yet they act like they're saving your life. Lifeguards are lifesavers – it's in their job title. And you see how they go about their work? Ripped and stripped to the waist in the brilliant sunshine, chatting up the pretty girls smoking French cigarettes on the beach. And they actually save lives. They save people from drowning, which, if you ask me, is a fate worse than death.

Friday 9th July

Twice I have been taken into hospital. Both times on a Friday. I am extra cautious on Fridays now. If I get to the end of a Friday and all is well, I think of myself as a lucky woman. Nothing untoward happened today. But then nothing that was toward anything happened either.

Sometimes I wish that someone would steal my identity online. They might do better than me! And if they struck up a promising relationship with an internet stranger but couldn't meet up in real life, as it would blow their cover, I would step in, say thank you very much, and take the dinner date on offer.

Saturday 10th July

I made cookies today and, halfway through, Spoiler Alert, I didn't have any chocolate for the chocolate chips. What I did have was a pack of very fine Green & Blacks chocolate biscuits, unopened since Christmas. So I broke these biscuits into the dough and made Chocolate Biscuit Chocolate Biscuits. My first actual invention. They cost about 68p each but are delicious.

Monday 12th July

It is someone's birthday today.

Rebecca Shackleton was my best friend. At least she was for two years, when we were both at sixth-form college. She was on a BTEC drama course and I was taking three A-levels in English, Maths and Chemistry. We were the same age. Both born in 1971 and her birthday was July 12th and mine was December 7th: 12/7 and 7/12. She was a punk. I was not. When I say punk, Becky was, more accurately, a post-punk. She had gothic tendencies, as we all did then, but she also liked The Cramps, The Ramones and Dead Kennedys. The closest I had gotten to any form of youth cult was crimping my hair for a Jesus and Mary Chain concert at the Guildhall. Some amazing bands came to the South Coast. I saw REM at the Guildhall, with Michael Stipe singing The Velvet Underground's *Pale Blue Eyes*. I saw Mudhoney and Nirvana (!!)

at the university. I always felt a bit sorry for the bands, though. No more or less sorry than I would feel for them when looking at their tour dates and seeing Lincoln or Hull, but none of these places are New York and CBGB's or London and The Marquee Club, are they? Anyway, Becky was a proper punk. Beautiful and dangerous. I would realise many years later that she looked like Edie Campbell. I didn't know what Edie Campbell looked like until, one day in WHSmith, I thought I saw Becky on the cover of *Vogue*. Becky was ridiculously pretty, but that went unrecognised by the boys at school and the local lads who jeered at her and only saw the heavy make-up and hair shaved on both sides. All I knew was that Becky looked like no one else I knew. She was a little bit Debbie Harry in *Videodrome* – not in looks so much but in feel, if that makes sense.

We were close back then, inseparable in term time, spending every evening together on our favourite bench. In the winter, when it was too cold for the park, we would spend hours and hours on the phone. We talked a lot. And then talked a lot more. We skipped college on sunny days and went to the coast; Becky always eating those green and white Twister ice lollies. There's nothing more British than a punk on a pier or a goth on the beach, is there? It was during this time that I failed my first driving test – by miles! I couldn't bear to leave the college common room, where I'd be chain-smoking and chatting with Becky and our friends, and I missed more than half of the driving lessons. I had to take the test on the date agreed because I couldn't bear to tell my dad that I had skipped all the lessons he'd paid for. I'm pretty sure it was a first for the test instructor to have someone who couldn't actually operate the pedals and gears before. I was failed in the test centre car park, he wouldn't let me out on the road.

This is all getting a little too like my life history and not at all what I meant to write. You have to 'be someone' to write a biography and I am not one. Stephen Hendry wrote his biography at the ridiculously young age of seventeen, but he had won the World Snooker Championship. I have achieved nothing of the sort. However, there was one incident with Becky that does deserve to be told in whatever book I am writing, because it just doesn't happen to everyone.

The year we finished college, when all our friends and enemies went off to university and I started out at the department store I still work at now, Becky dropped the punk look and persona completely and, huge shock, enrolled on a secretarial course! This transformation happened over the three-month summer break, when I was either at work or looking after my mother, and hadn't seen Becky at all, really. It was as much of a surprise to me as it was to everyone else. I just didn't know why she would do it. She could have gone to drama school. She could have just dropped out completely – in fact, that would have made more sense. There was a guy called Simon Locke, who never changed his clothes in sixth-form. His long, dyed-red hair went into dreadlocks from neglect rather than cultural appropriation. A travelling anti-cruise-missile festival called Torpedo Town set up camp near us that summer and he joined it, never to return. She could have done that.

But Becky, now officially Rebecca, really did clean up and go back to college for a one year secretarial course. I saw her a few times, in heels, a pencil skirt and a blouse with little flowers on it. She looked prettier than in her punk period. You could see the mole on her cheekbone that her greasepaint make-up had been covering. Of course I asked her, like, how could this happen? Just one big WHY? And then one night I got my answer. We were at a very bland and quiet pub in town, just the two of us, and she told me. She was going to get qualified and climb the ladder to become a PA to a Chief Executive and then defraud them of everything and leave the country. Word for word, that was her plan. I had never even had a hint of this in all the time I had known her. Seriously, where does that come from? I think I said 'Wow', certainly not 'Cool'. Then she told me she had a boyfriend that she hadn't told her mother about. He was older than her. And he had a van. The van seemed to have great significance. She said we should go to hers and she would show me something. So we did and, sitting in her bedroom, she told me that, over the summer, she and her secret boyfriend had held up a building society! They'd gotten away with a thousand pounds! I was just in total shock hearing all this. I don't remember saying anything. Then she said she'd show me what it was she was going to show me. From the bottom of her wardrobe, she brought out a shoebox from under two other shoeboxes. She opened the lid, took out some Converse trainers, and there it was – a gun. A gun!! A small black handgun. If anyone is reading this in America or, I don't know, Beirut, or even the South of England today, please understand, no one upon no one in my world had a gun. Much less a nineteen-year-old girl. I thought I knew her but, right then, I knew that I didn't. She suddenly seemed much older and much more real and I felt, for the first time, I think, much less real... like I was watching a film but the film was real life and I was in the audience.

We didn't see much of each other that year for the simple reason that neither of us contacted the other. Her secret was safe with me. I told no one. Even now I have changed her name for this book. But, come the following summer, Rebecca was gone. She sent me a card that I still have now, rabbits on the front and a forwarding address in Bracknell, Berkshire on the inside. That was it. I saw her mum a couple of times after that but she said she had lost contact with Rebecca too. Friends Reunited and MySpace and Facebook all came, one after the other, and each time I looked and didn't find her. She had completely disappeared. What was worse was that I hadn't gone anywhere. She could easily have found me. I never moved. I would have been the least-challenging case Interpol ever had. What that meant was that Becky didn't want to find me. She just didn't want to make contact. And didn't care.

Monday 19th July

Today I need to time think.

Thinking.

Thinking.

Sunday 25th July

I am going to write something now that I didn't expect to be writing when I started on this (lifesaving) book project. I have been trying to keep it simple: just the thoughts and ideas. Yes, some anecdotes and reminiscences have found their way in. They may still get edited out. I am aware of *The Diary of a Nobody*, though I haven't read it. That's not what I am writing. Although technically I am making diary entries, I really am only using the dates to show the frequency of the thoughts and ideas. This is not supposed to be my diary, or an autobiography or a novel. It is just a book. And I thought it might be an original book too – given that it is somewhat free of format and, as far as I am aware, any significant precedent. However, that is going to change. I have met someone. This only happened a week ago. Last Sunday it was. I was keeping them out of these pages. But as you will have noticed, that has kept me out of writing the book. I couldn't actually think of anything other than this person and, as a result, the writing stopped. The pages are blank, which is no good for anyone. I don't think I have much of a choice but to bring them into the story, and loosen up a bit while I am at it, something that has been incredibly hard to do these last few days.

A week ago, Sunday, I was up early and drove to the seafront. I was going to walk and sit on a bench and hopefully have some new thoughts. It can be cold in the mornings on the coast so I was wearing a hoodie that belonged to my eldest son. We have had half a wardrobe of his clothes left in the house since he went to university. I wear them, his younger brother wears them and my husband occasionally does too. It was before 9am, the sun was yet to burn off the clouds and I was walking through the chill air with my arms wrapped round me. A youth on a skateboard was headed in my direction. They passed by. There weren't many other people about. I carried on walking but heard the skateboard again, rolling closer up behind me, click-clacking over the paving. I turned round as they said: "Palace. That's a Palace hoodie." It was a girl speaking. She flipped up her board, catching it by the trucks underneath.

"Yes," I said. "It's my son's. Was his. I don't think he wants it any more." I knew it was a Palace hoodie. It had a huge triangle logo saying 'Palace' on the back.

"Cool Mom," the girl said, using the American pronunciation. She wasn't American but maybe these kids use 'Mom' now – or just speak that way when they want to.

"I want to skate for them," she added. She was pretty. A little bit tomboyish but, in a T-shirt, baggy jeans, sneakers, backpack and holding a skateboard, it's hard not to look that way. She had a nose stud, which was actually quite pretty too, certainly not offensive. Her hair was dark blonde and looked like it might have been cut back to the roots, having previously been dyed pink or green, or both. At least, so I surmised. I knew (from the internet) that the body sends the brain 11 million bits per second, but the mind can only process 50 bits per second. So I did the best I could to get a quick read of her.

"They have a skate team," she said. "A pro team, you

know, sponsored. That's what they do... skate for a living – professionally."

"And they have girls on the team?" I asked.

"No."

"Why not?"

"I don't know. Maybe no girl is good enough."

"It's early for a Sunday," I said. "Is that why you're out? Practicing?"

She shook her heard: "Going home. Crashed at a friends."

"Ah."

"Café is open, if you want to buy me breakfast."

I was surprised by this. "You're offering for me to buy you breakfast?"

"Got no money," she said with a shrug.

So I did buy her breakfast. Eggs and beans on toast with a large mug of tea. And she talked a lot. About her A-levels. About her parents. How she had moved to the area a few years ago from another similarly unspectacular place that was just like here. She had turned eighteen in January. She was waiting for her exam results but didn't really want to go to university. She wanted to skate. There was a picture of her in a skateboard magazine. She showed it to me on her phone and I put my glasses on to see it. She might move to London. She told me what bands she liked. She had met one of the singers from one of the bands. The local skate shop owner had asked if she would model some shirts for their website. It was a lot to listen to.

I didn't really talk about myself. Anything I might have said seemed boring to me before I said it. She asked a few questions. She didn't know my youngest son. They were the same age but had been to different schools and had no shared interests. She told me that her mother was a teacher and her dad worked in electronics for Marconi.

"Do you want another tea?" I asked.

"No. Thanks," she said, picking up her phone from the table. "I should go, really. What's your name?"

"June."

We hadn't even asked each other's names.

"That's a nice name. I'm Pipa," she said, before adding, "with only one P – in the middle – P-i-p-a – in case you put me in your book."

"In my book?" I was confused. "How did you know?"

Pipa looked at me like my sons often did, when I said I'd never seen *Star Wars* or that I was going to watch *Call of Duty* when I meant *Line of Duty*.

"You told me when we sat down!" Pipa said. "I asked what you did and you said you were writing a book."

"Did I?" I had forgotten.

"Tell me your number and I'll text you mine," Pipa said.

"Oh, right. OK. Hang on." I had come out without my phone. Just the little notepad and pen and my car keys in the pocket of the hoodie. "My phone must be in the car." I wrote the number down for her on a page and tore it out.

"Thank you for breakfast," Pipa said, picking up her skateboard and shuffling down the banquette to get out of the booth. "I'll text you."

I walked back to the car. The phone was in the side tray of the door. There was a new WhatsApp message.

I want to c u again, it read.

I drove home. Dealt with a few things. Sat in the garden. This is the start of the time when I was not writing. Not able to write. I looked at the message again. She'd have known I had seen it and read it when I first got to the car. Thank goodness WhatsApp doesn't show a blue tick for every time you read the same message without replying. The ticks would be in double figures by now. I went inside. Came out again. Unwound the hose and watered the plants. My husband was out all day at an athletics event. My youngest son only notionally lives at home with us now and I hadn't seen him for days. My neighbour Miriam was in her garden. The same Miriam who said she felt lucky not to win the lottery. Well, now she was lucky not to meet an eighteen-year-old skater girl who was hitting on her. And I know there is nothing I have written yet that suggests Pipa was a lesbian or, indeed, in any way attracted to me, but that's my failing as a writer, I'm afraid. I felt it. It just wasn't something I could find a way to explain. I could have said that she maintained eye contact with me for the whole time during breakfast but that's too obvious and also just not true – at one point she was looking at my hands. That was when she reached for her phone and I moved my hand, thinking she was going to touch it. We both noticed it. But even writing this now, I can tell you that it is coming out too clumsy. It was all a lot more subtle than that. The signals were imperceptible. There wasn't anyone else in the café. If there had been, trust me, they would not have thought 'Well, those two are going to have an affair.' They'd have thought I was her mother, that's what they would have thought. But the quantum mechanics were at work. Communication passed through the atoms that made up the table, the floor, the booth itself. Shapes made by Pipa's eyes and mouth were being received by my eyes and processed by the million, million receptors in my brain and passed back again.

Standing still in the garden, I had now flooded two plant pots. I turned off the hose and sat down with the phone. I was going to have to reply.

Let's do that, I wrote.

Then I saw the message was sent. And then read. And then, briefly, the brilliant 'Typing...', which could have been my status for the last three months.

GREAT! When next day off?

Wednesday.

I know where we can go. Pick me up. Sending address.

What time? I wrote.

Then the address arrived. Somewhere I knew fairly well. Nice houses on that street.

11am.

The rest of Sunday, and then Monday and Tuesday at work, were spent thinking, contemplating the impossible, asking myself a question I couldn't answer... What the fuck should I wear? It was a very good question. We had met by virtue of the accidental and inappropriate (for me) Palace sweatshirt. My son had passed through that phase quickly and there was just that one hoodie. Plus it was forecast to be warm and sunny. The wolves howling at the moon T-shirt was definitely taking the teenage look too far – literally like a sheep (mutton) in wolf's clothing. Dungarees or a jumpsuit (both of which I do own) would have been a very clichéd lesbian look and, I know this is ridiculous in this context, but if there is one thing I am not, it's a lesbian. Besides, dungarees are crazy hard to get off in a hurry (if I were to do any same-sexing).

Wednesday morning, after my husband had gone to work, I sat on our bed in my bra and knickers and looked at myself in the mirror. It wasn't my forty-nine-year-old body that shook me. It was, rather, the ever-so-hopeful look on my face. Honestly, I could break my own heart. I'll write that again because I don't think I have ever read it before: I could break my own heart. It just hit me. Completely undid me. I'd made this up. Of course I had made it up. I had written it into existence, probably because I realised that the book needed it to happen. Just writing down thoughts and ideas wasn't going to be enough; it was too disjointed and needed an emotional pull. It needed what authors, or the people who take money off wannabe-writers, call a story arc. Well, it proved one thing, I was getting better as a writer, I had fooled myself. I had made myself believe it, and now I was embarrassed. Looking in the mirror, I could see myself embarrassed. But also relieved. Relieved that I had found out now, saving myself further embarrassment later. Getting dressed was suddenly a whole lot easier. White blouse, jeans and the Balenciaga belt. Phone and lip gloss went into my purse. My hair, which had also been the subject of too much speculation and prevarication, was now quickly pulled into a ponytail. Driving round to Pipa's address, I laughed out loud. It had been a weird week. Three days of mental gymnastics and emotional contortion. But I was mightily relieved. I was an idiot. A deluded almost-fifty-year-old idiot. But I was happy. And I laughed at myself again.

I turned into her street and started looking for the house number. I needn't have bothered. Pipa was standing on her doorstep and came skipping down to the car. I didn't even turn the engine off. "Drive round the corner," she said. "Stop here." I pulled the car over by a postbox.

"Do you need to post a letter?" I asked.

"That's funny way to put it," she said. She hadn't even seen the postbox. "Maybe I have to lick a stamp first."

I looked at her. Nose stud, earrings, vest top. She was looking at me too.

"You look sexy," she said.

I thought:

Oh dear

Oh dear

Oh dear

Oh, what the hell.

And I kissed her.

The place Pipa knew where we could go was a forest, about a twenty-minute drive away. We didn't talk much during the drive. We arrived there and parked. It was mercifully quiet. The weather was so good that most people would have headed to the beach. Pipa grabbed the rucksack she had thrown in the back. "I brought some water and a blanket," she said. "And apples," she added, after checking the bag. This was novel. Twenty-four years of being a parent and someone young enough to be my child had packed provisions for a picnic. All I had was a lip gloss. We walked into the woods. We walked a long way into the woods. She stopped and kissed me twice. The sub-atomic particles in my panties (I never say panties – always knickers, but the alliteration, you know) went into a frenzy of nuclear fusion, like I had the Hadron Collider between my legs. I struggled on. We reached a small clearing of ferns. There was enough sun for it to be warm. Pipa put the blanket down, unbuttoned my blouse and then... she made love to me. I did things to her too, but truly she made love to me.

We got dressed, ate our apples and shared the water. I said I needed to go and pee. Pipa said I didn't need to go anywhere. "Just go over there," she said, pointing to an area of the clearing a few yards away. So I did. She wasn't watching but she was still talking to me. The strange thing was that peeing in plain sight and such close proximity to someone else felt more bizarre and brazen to me than the sex that had preceded it.

We drove back into town, chatting more easily now. I was telling her about Becky and the gun in the shoebox.

"Let's stop," Pipa said, seeing a service station ahead. "Now I need to pee and they have a Costa."

So we stopped and I bought two lattes while she went to the bathroom.

"We can sit in and drink them," Pipa said, when she returned. "I don't want to get back too soon," she added, touching my hand.

"OK," I said. We weren't all over each other like a young couple. We were just together. Again, no doubt, looking to all the world like mother and daughter. This was just as well as the minute we sat down I looked up and saw Len coming out of the men's toilets. You had to pass the Costa Coffee to get out to the car park. He was headed our way.

"Pipa," I whispered, with some urgency. "Someone I know."

"Hello, June," said Len, standing very tall above us, smiling and taking his hand quickly away from his fly. He had been struggling with the zipper and it hadn't made it all the way up to full closure.

"Hello, Len," I said. "This is..."

Pipa turned her head to greet Len. He recoiled.

"Oh, I... didn't know you two knew each other," Len said. He looked awkward now. I don't know how I was looking, but he was surely the more uncomfortable.

Pipa was quickest to say something: "We only just met. I was friends with June's son." Pipa, of course, didn't know my son or even his name but that didn't seem to matter to Len. He was the one who was desperate to get away.

"Right," said Len. "Well, beautiful day. Don't want to miss any sun."

Len walked briskly away and out into the car park.

"How do you know Mr Simmonds?" Pipa asked.

"Mr Simmonds?" Peg and Len's surname was Hutchins. "I am not so sure that I do now," I said. "How do you know him?"

"He was the woodwork teacher at my old school," said Pipa.

We sat for a little longer in Costa, explaining to each other what we knew about Len and Mr Simmonds. We ran through dates and places too on the drive back. Parked up around the corner from her house, we came to the conclusion that one of two things must be going on:

1) The Len I knew was substituted in the hospital for the Mr Simmonds Pipa knew. This was still considered the least likely explanation, mainly because, as far as we knew, things like this just didn't happen. Aside from Peggy having a much nicer husband than the one who might otherwise be dead, there wasn't much of a motivation for Mr Simmonds to become Len Hutchins, seeing as how Peg, to be perfectly honest, was a bit of a nightmare to live with.

2) The Len I knew of old was either a bigamist – Pipa couldn't remember if he was married when she knew him – or, at the very least, led a double life. Very few people knew what went on in the naval base where he worked. It had big gates and you had to clock in. Wives couldn't just pop round with their husbands' lunches. It was possible that Len pretended to work there and actually drove a hundred miles each way to work as a woodwork

teacher in a city comprehensive school on another part of the south coast. Maybe. Only maybe. And that theory would rely on the vegan diet transformation. And it was a little problematic, as Pipa didn't remember him as being particularly leery, and said he had no reputation for being anything other than very nice.

It was getting late in the evening now, so Pipa jumped out of the car and skipped off round the corner to her family home. I drove back to mine. That night I read back over the book so far and, on my list of possible new experiences, added 'watch this space', in italics after Amateur Detective. I did not add the new experiences of 'Lesbian Sex' or 'Openly Peeing In Front of Someone' to the list because that would spoil the surprise. Pipa, by the way, has never had proper restaurant sushi either and is keen to try it too. Late in the night I was still feeling an excess of sexiness so I woke my husband up and gave him something else to think about other than his athletics team.

In all, the greatest of days.

Monday 26th July

'The funny thing about regret is: it is always better to regret something you have done than something you haven't done.'

That's a quote from the spoken introduction to the Butthole Surfers song *Sweat Loaf*, itself a cover of Black Sabbath's *Sweet*

Leaf. I still play the song now, along with The Cure, Pixies, The Breeders, The Smiths and The Jesus And Mary Chain. My music tastes from 1986–1988, when I was fifteen to seventeen, have been set in stone ever since. They are all still my favourites. I am telling you now not because I regret the actions of last week – far from it – more because, as promised, I have loosened up a bit. I wanted to tell you that when I drove the school run back in the early 2000s, my eldest boy would make me play this song over and over. The next lines of the spoken intro are;

'By the way, if you see your mom this weekend be sure and tell her... SATAN, SATAN, SATAN!'

Then the huge Sabbath guitar riff kicks in. One day we gave a lift to a quiet boy whose mum taught cello. This boy also had a violin case, I remember. I played the 'SATAN, SATAN, SATAN' as requested and heard my son (all of five or six years old) say to the other boy: "I bet your mum likes Dido."

Pipa and I are obviously not going to fall in love and live happily ever after. I mean, don't be ridiculous (June). We are, however, going to spend next weekend in an Airbnb in London. I have booked one on Wardour Street, right above a Ben & Jerry's, a stone's throw from the skate shop Supreme, an Olympian stone's throw from the Palace shop, and right round the corner from Old Compton Street, where all the gay bars are. This is not exactly what I have told my husband. I told him I was going to Guildford, after seeing Peggy's photos, to do some shopping and also some writing, hence needing to spend two nights away. The subject of what I am writing and the question of why I am writing has come up recently. It's kind of a shame as, up until last week, I could have asked him to read it and spot any typos. Now, because of Pipa, it is all going to have to be part of a much bigger conversation scheduled for... later.

Tuesday 27th July

Len is now impossible to bump into. Peggy assures me he has not gone into hiding. He has just 'been busy'. "He has installed a bird table in the garden," she tells me. I thought about his woodwork teaching. "Installed or built from scratch?" I asked, much to Peg's consternation. "He brought it back from the garden centre," she said. "I'd love to see it," I ventured further. Peggy shut this right down. "Well, I am sure it will be there next year," she said, by way of underlining that her annual invitation to visit was just as it was described.

This afternoon a young male librarian told me my name was the same as Helmut Newton's wife's name. This is true but not something anyone I know seems to know. On the rare occurrences it does come up, it is usually the result of someone Googling me, which always begs the question: why? I mean I have known my neighbour Miriam for ten years and never looked her up on the internet. Anyway, this young photography fan at the library didn't have time to Google my name. He just saw my card and said it. I think I may have blushed. He certainly caught me off guard. I said, "It's true." And then for some reason added, "I have the same name as me."

That could be another title for this book.

JUNE NEWTON

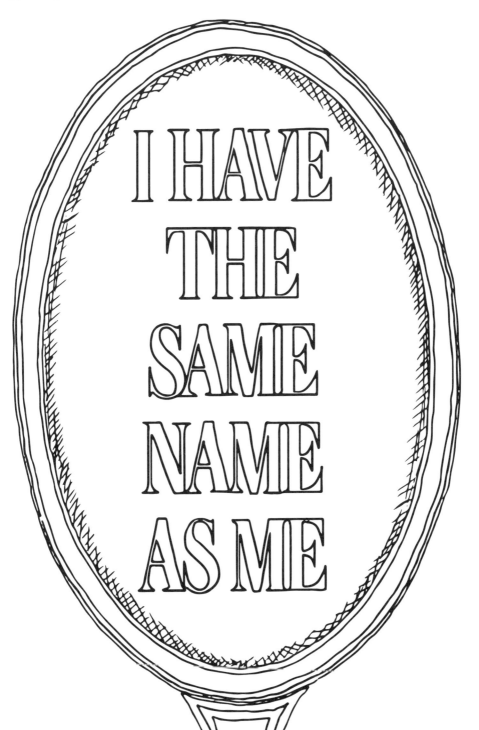

I HAVE THE SAME NAME AS ME

Wednesday 28th July

Pipa has been WhatsApping me today. She has been sleuthing. Texting and calling old school friends from her hometown.

Mr Simmonds first name was/is Chris. Married. One grown-up son. Pipa x

And then another an hour later.

Wife died. Two years ago.

Suddenly I am full of ideas and desperate to write them all down. I am sure these are all thoughts I have had or half-had over the years and never quite formulated into concepts. There was no outlet, no impetus like I have now. None of them have anything to do with bigamy or lesbianism. The sex has turned my brain on! These are just some of the things I have scrambled to write down today. Excuse the randomness but this is an outpouring of relief! I have numbered them so you don't get lost.

1. The annual incomes of the world's one hundred richest people could end global poverty four times over, at least, so I read. Inspired by this, I thought that if George Clooney and Robert Redford could share their disproportionate good looks and charm around equally, it would make every man on the planet just that little bit more likeable.

2. Heard someone say 'sands of time' today. I think it's the title of a computer game and nothing to do with hourglasses or egg timers. There must be lots of things that are more popular in analogous form than in real life. You don't see so many pairs of rose-tinted glasses. We don't sell them in our store. How many more metaphoric safety nets are there than real ones in the world? I saw Cirque du Soleil once and they didn't even use one. On the other hand, when my husband has cricket on the radio, I have heard commentators use the phrase 'corridor of uncertainty'. I like the idea of it, but I don't imagine it is more useful than a real corridor, which are almost essential in a hotel, they save everyone from walking through everyone else's rooms.

3. I can't seem to Google anyone without seeing their net worth. 'What's Julia Louis-Dreyfus' net worth?' 'What's Jean-Michel Jarre's net worth?' It's everywhere. 'What's a fisherman's net worth?' I want to know.

When my thoughts read back like jokes, does that make them any less valid?

4. The women that say they have buried three husbands... but what if one of them had *actually* buried one. For real.

5. Big data and statistics. You get them on everything. There are still things I'd like to know: like what's the balance between the numbers of people described as having animalistic qualities

and the numbers of personified animals? You know, for every Richard the Lionheart, there is a Mister Ed. I imagine it is a perfect state of equilibrium, a previously undiscovered rule of the universe.

6. There should be special casts or slings or crutches (bright red ones, perhaps) for people with conditions you can't see. Colleagues would make a fuss over them, friends would sign their cast. I'd sign the cast of a friend with, say, sleep apnea – quite happily.

7. Secret billionaire. That's what I am with these thoughts. When this book comes out, that's what they'll say: "I worked with June for eight years and I would never have guessed. You wouldn't know, to look at her. All that time and, who knew, that when it came to ideas and insights, she was one of the richest women in the world?"

There's more! But I will stop now. I am exhausted. It is nearly 2am.

Thursday 29th July

Very long phone call with Pipa tonight. My husband was out. My phone timed the call at a few minutes over four hours. It was like being a teenager again. It was certainly exactly like being *with* a teenager again. Of course, this was a WhatsApp call and therefore didn't cost either of us anything. I used to make similarly telemarathonic calls when I was Pipa's age and then suffer the wait until the end of the month when the BT bill came through the letterbox and all hell broke loose. If that was on the same day as the pickle jar running dry, I could be grounded. My sons and Pipa and her friends have it easy by comparison. They have headphones too, so they can text chat with one friend – more than one friend – while speaking to the other, like they are receptionists in *The Man From U.N.C.L.E.* It has all moved on so fast. I remember when my eldest first discovered FaceTime and would leave the laptop open in the lounge, while setting up his action figures. I would come in and nag at him to clear up the crisp packets and sweet wrappers and I'd hear a little voice saying: "I can't see. Your mum is in the way." Then I'd run into whoever it was's mother at the school gates and be told that I really should put some clothes on when walking around the house. It freaks me out now when I see toddlers in pushchairs with iPads. It's the strangest technology: only babies and grandparents seem to use them. Unless you consider nappies and incontinence pants as the same thing, I can't think of another product that appeals almost exclusively to both extremes of the age spectrum.

This was all discussed with Pipa in the four-hour call. A lot of the references had to be explained and I probably overused prefaces like 'You won't remember this but...' but she didn't seem to mind. It was good to talk – ironically, another BT advert reference she wouldn't know, spoken originally by Bob Hoskins, who she also wouldn't know. That would mean she hadn't seen *Mona Lisa* or *The Long Good Friday*, which we could watch together. And she probably hadn't seen *The Crying Game* either, which I don't think Bob Hoskins was in, but I am just reminded of now. She wouldn't even know about the 'don't tell anyone' surprise ending.

I played true or false band names with her. That is something I used to do with my sons and their friends – but I didn't tell her that. I gave her Orchestral Manoeuvres In The Dark, Living In A Box, Gaye Bykers On Acid and New Fast Automatic Daffodils. I didn't even have to make any up. She didn't know Pet Shop Boys or Katrina And The Waves were real. Of course my trick is to pause between each word so that it seems like I'm making it up as I go along. When she learnt that tactic, I sped up and caught her on the double bluff.

The most minutes of the call were spent discussing Len. Free or not, these were minutes I would gladly have paid premium rates for. What incredible fun to have a real life and, quite possibly, life or death mystery to share – so early in our relationship too! Pipa had her laptop open – hopefully not texting other friends – she promised me she wasn't. Anyway, she was on Google answering the questions that I was asking: "If he was a bigamist, don't they usually have the same job but two different wives and families?"

I could hear Pipa typing.

"There's one here who was a doctor. He was the same doctor to both wives, they just didn't know about each other. And this one claimed to be a CIA agent seconded to MI5. He had three wives in the UK and thirteen kids."

"Three families," I said. "We only know about two of Len's. He might have more. We don't know how big of a bigamist he is. In these cases, none of the women knew, right?"

"Looks that way. Do you think someone might be married and know that their husband is also married to someone else?" Pipa asked.

"Peggy gave me a look that was definitely keep-your-nose-out-of-it. And she's been evasive lately."

"She may have found out when he had the heart attack."

"Two next of kins."

"Yeah. His other wife was already dead, though."

"But the son."

"Ah. Yes."

I asked Pipa if there was anything to be found out about bigamists having completely different personalities for their different lives.

"Not that I can see. The wives here are generally reporting similar behaviour. Unsurprisingly, their main complaint was that their husbands went AWOL for weeks at a time."

"Len had the perfect excuse for that; telling Peg he was in the merchant navy, that can be months at sea."

"Maybe whole term times."

"Yes! I need to somehow check if Len's Peggy-time coincided with school holidays."

And so it went on. And on. Pictures of Len/Chris were found amongst school-year group photos that were online. Records were discovered showing registrations of the two marriages.

"We can't actually do anything with this information, though, can we?" Pipa said, near to the end of the call. "It's illegal but not really harming anyone now."

She was right. Take Pipa and me, for example. Even if someone found out about us, and our relationship was not even illegal remember, we still wouldn't appreciate them going public with the information. Exposing Len was only going to cause hurt, even if, as I suspected, Peggy already knew. What I really wanted to do was speak to Len. If I could get a message to him that his secret was safe with me, then he could be the one person I could tell about Pipa. He wouldn't expose me, as I had the bigger scoop. The new Len was fun to talk to. And I was itching to tell someone about Pipa (well, really about myself and not about Pipa at all, but you know what I mean). It had only been ten days and even with all this writing about it, the secret was burning away inside me.

Friday 30th July

Pipa and I met at the station and took the train to London, as planned. We walked along the Thames from London Bridge. I can't begin to describe the scene on the South Bank or the enormous street party we walked into, and tried to sleep through, in Soho. Pipa had been up for Pride a few years before and said it wasn't much more crowded then. I mean I could describe what we saw – it would take a very long time but I could do it. What I couldn't describe was what I felt. I had never learned the words I would need to explain my responses. The dictionary I have at home wouldn't do it. I'd need one of those multivolume sets from the library. And no wonder Peggy never came up here. She'd have had a heart attack, like her husband, before she'd gotten out the other side of Borough Market. Pipa has been trying to help, telling me to take notes of this or to remember that, but her most amazing moments are not mine. She could have written a book about the skaters on the South Bank by the National Film Theatre. That is where Palace first started, I now know. She's going back there tomorrow or Sunday. I will happily go with her because I am sure that part of the river is where a scene in *Truly, Madly, Deeply* was filmed and I could stand in that spot forever.

Sex tonight. Another contender for the title of this book.

SEX TONIGHT

BY
JUNE NEWTON

Saturday 31st July

Pipa and I had breakfast in Balans on Old Compton Street, lunch at Rose Bakery in Dover Street Market and tonight we are going to eat real sushi – Michelin-starred sushi, no less, at AMA in Mayfair. AMA is very expensive and I have already bought Pipa a Palace shirt from the basement in Dover Street Market. Tomorrow's meals will have to be on a budget. Not that that is such a problem: too much choice is the problem. The Italian deli I Camisa, the fish and chip shop next door, The India Club on the Strand that, I just read, may have to close down, Joe Allen's, Maison Bertaux, Bruno's across the street, Lina Stores, Kettner's, Whole Foods, Gail's Bakery, Pizza Express with the live jazz music. Why are there only three meals in the day? Whose stupid idea was that? Bloody hell, even Pret A Manger at the station was a treat for us.

They have urinals on the street here. And portaloos for women, I should add. The urinals, though: open for all to see! I told Pipa that my first husband would have made a point of using one, even if he didn't need to pee. He drunkenly urinated into a Dyson Airblade. That is not something you need to do twice. He was actually really good like that; he always had to try anything new. I don't know how he would manage now, though, in his medieval battledress. You probably have to plan out toilet visits when you spend a night in shining armour. Pipa told me that her dad has a story of going to the loo in Trader Vic's in London. He was standing at the urinal with an unlit cigarette in his mouth and the bathroom attendant stepped up and lit it for him while he was peeing. That's classy. She also told me that her dad once dropped a weekly travelcard into the urinal and had to pick it out and dry it off, as it was only Tuesday and still worth about £20. That's too much information. Her dad must be great fun at a dinner party. Not that I can take great exception: my grandmother on my mother's side was obsessive about public toilets. She knew them all, their pros and cons. She shopped in BHS but used the loos in John Lewis. There were innumerable cafés she couldn't visit at all. There would be women's loos on TripAdvisor if she was still around. Most tourist attractions were out, unless it was National Trust. She raved about the bathrooms at Chatsworth House, until it was pointed out to her that the public toilets were in the visitor centre.

Pipa has gone round to the Palace store while I take a minute to type some of this up. Earlier today we walked past Alan Carr, the comedian and television presenter. And we saw Howard Jacobson, although only I recognised him (and we did have to Google 'bearded British authors' and find a picture of him to be sure). He probably lives on Meard Street, the short narrow lane on which our flat is on the corner; it looked like a house he was entering with his small bag of shopping. I also stood for a good fifteen minutes opposite The Groucho Club and watched people going in and out. There was no one I recognised, which does rather underline that I am not a member of that club; they all seemed to know each other. Now, though – a text. A WhatsApp from Pipa: *Bill Nighy is sitting outside Lina Stores on Brewer Street.* I am typing this half an hour later, by the way. The second I saw that message, I was up on my feet and out the door.

Oh Lord! AMA was another world. The name sounds like a *Doctor Who* planet – and it is one, it even has a science fiction door that we, more like Muppets, couldn't find and then couldn't open. But you walk inside to a chorus of 'Irasshaimase!' And, yes, I did have to ask the waiter to write that down for me. The restaurant was so welcoming. I mean I guess it should be at £250 for two. If I was mega-rich, like everyone else in there tonight, I would eat there every day. I'm too new to sushi and sashimi, Japanese beers and rice wines, to tell you what we ate, but the menu is online and, between the two of us, we ate most of it.

There were kids hanging out on the curb outside Supreme when we walked back from dinner. They are there now, as I write this, drinking and smoking weed and skating, grinding the kerb very loudly. We can see them from the apartment. There are two girls among them. Pipa says she recognises one of the Palace team too. I urge her to go down and introduce herself. She is reluctant. I ask if she can do the tricks they are trying to do. Pipa says she can. Go on then, I tell her. My sons would be the same – always were the same. I'd push them toward other boys on the street and they'd come cowering back: "Mum, you don't understand. They're drug dealers with knives. That's a gang. We can't just wander up and say hi." It's funny now to think I could be so clueless. I just always wanted them to have friends, not be left out. "Anyway, they're too young for me," I remember my son concluding, not realising the irony of his reasoning. I turned back to Pipa. "Get out there, will you? I'm not telling you again." She went and I was right, she fitted straight in. She drank and smoked and skated a bit and swapped numbers at the end. She told me this when she came back, thrilled and buzzing. I hadn't sat watching from the window like the pushy mums at the swimming baths. She was not my daughter and I was not pushy. I had a shower and lay on the bed.

Sex tonight.

Sunday 1st August

Sunday morning. A quarter to ten. I am sitting at the open window of our flat, two floors up on the corner of Wardour Street and Meard Street, and can hear four, maybe five, conversations on the street below. It's warm already. There are delivery men bringing Amazon boxes and packages from Matches and Mr Porter. Two very loud motorbikes pass by. I hear two different sirens at the same time: an ambulance that screams beneath me and then, seconds later, a fire engine following. Pigeons are on street cleaning duty. One, attempting to pick up a scrap, flicks it into the path of another, setting off what looks, from my vaunted vantage point, like a game of playground pigeon football. Pipa has encouraged me to write this piece, by the way. I said it's not going to be *Ulysses* or *Under Milkwood*. Thankfully she hasn't read either of them in part (like me) or in full. I will keep it in the present tense.

Quiet now and just the whirl of bicycle wheels as a Deliveroo delivery courier cycles the wrong way down the street. Then a man coughs, clearing his throat loudly. That sets a small dog barking. A girl is locking up her bicycle, which triggers an alarm on a bike beside it. They have alarms on bikes in Soho! Heavy rumbling engine sounds as a procession of food trucks and an articulated lorry follow a differently pitched but equally noisy street-cleaning vehicle. What must this place be like on a Monday morning? I wish I could be here to find out. Opposite, Peter Street basks in brilliant sunshine at the intersection with Walker's Court and disappears in equally strong shade at our end. The shop GCDS has the biggest sign and the least amount of customers. We didn't see one person go in all day yesterday. And it's next door to Supreme with its too, too long queue. Just proves, I suppose, that there are winners and losers, even here in the centre of the universe. Uber Eats and more Deliveroo cycle couriers lean on their bikes outside Bruno's café. Violent fashions pass below, worn by what I guess must be tourists. Within my line of sight, there are people in singlets and shorts and others wrapped up in coats. Howard Jacobson and his wife appear again and drop off a rubbish bag by the bins. There are two bags there now. When we arrived last night there were twenty or more – and a rat. The Jacobsons cross the road and slowly, very slowly, disappearing and reappearing as they make their way through the light and shade of Peter Street. The trundling sound of a wheel-along suitcase suddenly ceases as another tourist, a young woman, stops to get directions on her phone. I can hear the app's voice telling her to take a right at Meard Street. Children's voices climb sharply up to the window, calling out the names 'Ben' and 'Jerry' as they read the shop signage beneath me. A walking-tour guide is telling a couple they should wait just a minute to see if anyone else is joining them. Quiet again for a moment as someone cycles along, sitting upright in the saddle with their arms folded. I see the sun reflecting on the bald head of an old man below. He is dressed in layers of beige and is passed by a young man in a beige shirt with a beige jacket tied round his waist. A man carrying a puppy walks alongside his son, who, with straight blond hair to his jawline, looks like the boy from *Paris, Texas*. Builders are working at the end of Peter Street, adjacent to the graffiti-fronted building that brings the road to a full stop. A middle-aged man with a pink mohican and orange hi-vis jacket cycles up to the junction and looks both ways, up and down the one-way street. Very wise, I think, before he heads off the wrong way down it. And, above all this, the sky-blue sky.

Church bells peel for ten o'clock. Gay guys in outfits I don't have the time or turn of phrase to attempt to describe wander past. The boy and his father sit down outside Bruno's and arm wrestle on the very wobbly table, while the puppy looks up from a chair of its own. I can almost hear what they are saying but it is lost as the Bruno's waiter is talking Italian to someone, maybe everyone. A young, possibly Korean, man approaches down Peter Street with two bright yellow Selfridges bags. What time do they open? Another waiter from Bruno's smokes in the doorway of 101 Wardour Street. A young couple peer into the windows of Supreme and are given some, no doubt unhelpful, information by a security guard, who has just appeared on the scene. An Uber pulls up and more Chinese or Korean kids climb out in bucket hats and beanies. A Bruno's chef in an apron is now also smoking outside, around the corner from the waiter – either they are not friends or they have just seen enough of each other already this morning. A sleek black Jaguar convertible turns into Peter Street and parks. I watch as the mechanical roof slowly puts itself up. A girl with long blonde hair, wearing a deep V-neck cricket sweater and ever-so-short skirt appears below me. It's not a good look. I can see straight down the sweater and she has nothing on underneath. Someone's fantasy call girl, I guess. There isn't time to tell Pipa to come and see her as seconds later an Uber pulls up and she is whisked away.

Again I wonder, what must the scene be like on a working weekday? Another father and son come out of Bruno's. I have long lost count of the people I have seen. Everything I have described can be multiplied five times over, in reality. It is now a quarter past ten. And quiet again. For a full ten seconds. Then the music starts from a bar down the road. A woman, who may once have been a man, is hollering in a very loud, probably fake, New York accent about jail time. She is giving the Bruno's crowd a fashion show from a few yards off the curb and into the road. A van driver makes a point of stopping and beeping at her, which triggers a torrent of wildly abusive language. She takes off a shoe and attacks the front of the van with it. I'm hardly a local resident but even I have lived here long enough (two nights) to know he should have just driven around her. The woman walks away, still shouting, while the Bruno's waiters call after her, wishing her well in their accented English. Then Pipa appears at the one free table outside the café and is waving at me. I do a double take and look behind me into the kitchenette, where I thought she was. She's brilliant, that girl. I flip the lid of the laptop down, tuck it under my arm and skip/trip down the hallway stairs to join her.

Now I can see all the way up Meard Street and, even with its curve (back in time), I can still see a narrow sliver of Dean Street. I can also see all the way down Wardour Street to the iridescent red lanterns hanging across the pedestrianised part of Chinatown. With this longer perspective, I realise that there are a hundred or more people on the street and really I had done well to describe any of them because these hundred people are constantly changing places, swapping out of the scene with new people. It's like when the old departure boards at airports would update themselves in real time. But this never stops. It just shuffles and reshuffles itself.

"You look happy," says Pipa. And I am happy. It is almost 11am already. The time in my life when time passed the quickest is here and now, when more happens in one moment than I can possibly write down. There is also more litter than I can possibly pick up. I would have to learn to let that go if I lived here.

I order a cheese and pickle toasted sandwich. Nothing wrong with that for breakfast. Pipa has the same order of beans and egg on toast and mug of tea that I bought her when we first met. As the waiter brings the food, I notice another café over the road called Cheez & Toast! It is closed, though, and looks like it is boarded up.

"You put them out of business," I say to the waiter, the same one that I had heard shouting Italian before.

"Them? They never really opened. Just for one week, I think."

"Money laundering," a voice from behind me says. I look round to see a man unlocking the door of 101. I also note the 'No Smoking' signs. I had lost count how many people had stood there smoking after the Bruno's waiter.

"I went in there," the man says. "I looked up at the menu on the board behind the counter and it was just horrible. Horribly complicated. Stilton on olive bread, that kind of thing. All the bread had seeds or herbs in it. And I did try to order. I picked the plainest most bread-like bread and then I asked for cheddar, which they had to go and find somewhere out the back. But then I just thought I had better ask if the pickle was Branston because, you know, that could be awful if it wasn't, and the guy serving me just looked blank. I said the word 'pickle' again. You do have pickle? He went out the back again, where the kitchen presumably was, talked to someone, and then the boss or the owner or whoever he was, came out and said, 'No pickle.'"

The man in the door of 101 gestures across the road again where we could also see the signage. "It's called Cheez & Pickle!"

he says in exasperation.

"And you think money launderers?" I ask.

"Got to be," he replies, and opens the door to his building.

I look at my toasted sandwich. It looks like Branston.

"Here, we have pickle," says our waiter, proudly. "Branston pickle. Big, big jar." He says this while holding his hands wide apart for us to marvel at the industrial catering-sized jar he is miming.

I'm sitting, writing, in the small churchyard-slash-park opposite the *Les Mis* mural on Wardour Street. Pipa is sharing a cigarette with a skater girl she met last night. A man, balding and overweight, wearing a black T-shirt and black jeans, sits on the bench next to me and makes a phone call.

"I'm in the park. I ate my lunch really quickly. I don't know if I told you but I bought three prawn curries from Tesco for £6.29. I had one last night and one today and I squashed one into your freezer. Because, you know, if I am ever there – it's a £2 meal. What? Oh, sorry. I did tell you. I forgot."

This is not a book-worthy eavesdrop but that's precisely why I am including it. Clearly not every Soho conversation is about the latest fashion party or an option on a TV series.

The flat was booked for three nights; that was the minimum so I had to take it. Pipa and I could stay tonight but that will also be problematic for me with work in the morning. I really shouldn't do it. It hasn't stopped me checking the trains, though, and there are a couple early enough for me to make it. I've been checking other things too, like how long, at £125 a night, I could live here before I ran out of money. This is a scenario where I give up my job, sell the house, take my half share of the small equity we have built up, and do nothing but write when I get here. A year is the answer, give or take being able to afford to buy the boys birthday and Christmas presents. Of course £125 a night is higher than I need to be paying. I could rent a studio apartment for less than that. So maybe it could be stretched to eighteen months. And then I could find work here. Selfridges seem to be doing well. Work three days a week part-time and this London life of mine could last two or three years. Not too bad. People have cancer prognoses shorter than that.

We do stay the third night. Sex again. Why not again?!

Monday 2nd August

I took the earliest train back on my own and left Pipa sleeping. I was at work before she got out of the bed and messaged me. Last night Pipa said I was getting good at sex. Admittedly this was in response to me asking her if I was doing it right. She said: "It's easy. You know the phrase 'to rub someone up the wrong way'? Well, just don't do that. Rub them up the right way."

This is a coming of age story, isn't it? Albeit that age is going to be fifty.

My lunch break was spent sitting on what would have been a bench in the precinct outside our store but is now a wooden armchair. The council have introduced a cluster of them facing each other. They are not wholly uncomfortable.

"So would you describe yourself as a lesbian now?" asked Jennifer, everyone's favourite psychologist from *The Sopranos*. She twitched her nose and her glasses did a little bunny hop.

"Me? No, not at all. I am a woman who had sex with a woman... *is* having sex with a woman."

"How is it?" Jennifer asked.

I wasn't expecting that question. "How is it? How is it for me, do you mean? Or 'how is it?' as in 'what is it like?'"

"I'm not sure. I'm just interested."

"You haven't tried it?"

"No."

"Ok. Well it's... good."

"Maybe it is something I could try... with you."

"That would be... something," I managed to say. "I think it's better when one of the two people is actually a lesbian."

"Oh," Jennifer said.

"I can get myself into the positions, but Pipa knows the proper names for them... If it was me and you, we might just start giggling."

"I can see that," Jennifer agreed. "There is a mental switch that can turn erotic and stimulating touch into something that is, well, best described as ticklish."

"Also I am not technically available, am I? I have a girlfriend."

"And you are married."

"True. I am doubly, definitely not available."

"Some people might think that having a female lover and a husband could be seen to negate the exclusivity of either relationship."

"You could see it that way," I said.

"I am also a lot older, of course, than you remember me from the 2000s."

"Ah, yes, I wasn't honestly thinking about that though. Really hadn't crossed my mind."

"But now that it has?"

"Now that it has... You want me to be honest?"

"Yes. Please," Jennifer said.

"I would definitely be more interested in *Sopranos* Season One Jennifer."

The Debenhams in town closed today. It has been scheduled for closure for a while. It was still a sad day. There are some towns and even cities on the south coast without any department stores now. Portsmouth lost three: Landports, Knight and Lee in Southsea, and their own Debenhams, earlier this year. Every time, the local news is the same. They have someone who has worked in the store for thirty years, usually in haberdashery, on the TV report, saying how they knew it was coming but it was still such a shock and what chance do they have now at finding another job. If you are reading this book, anytime a few years from now, then the chances are this has already happened to me.

I shall wear the wolves howling at the moon T-shirt on doomsday. That is an absolute promise!

I wonder, if this book does get published, if I'll get review quotes or endorsements from other authors on the back? I would like that. Everyone reads them, don't they? When I was very young, I saw one I will never forget. It was on the back of a Michael Palin book of *Ripping Yarns*, I think. It read:

'I couldn't put it down.'

Adhesive Weekly

That is still ever so funny. I don't suppose you are allowed to request them or write them yourself but I would like...

'She writes like an angel.'

Tuesday 3rd August

Pipa says she is thinking of getting her tongue pierced. She says I would like it. This, I could tell, was meant in a sexual way. She said it with what would have been a wink, if she could wink, which she can't, she just blinks with both eyes. She can't do the semi-colon text emoji – her wink is like this :

Seeing as how this book is steadily and irrevocably being dragged downstream by the faster running river of biography, I have decided to list all the people that are in my life but will not, I repeat, will not appear (or, in some cases, reappear) in these pages. I don't want people to think I don't have parents. I just don't want anyone to think about them or know what I think about them. So, the list;

My mother and my father. They are both alive and not well. They are a big part of my life. I see them regularly. Do I want to write about them? No thank you.

My brother. I don't see him so often. He's no stranger to me but he is stranger than me. Personality-wise he is another book altogether, preferably one not written by me.

My first husband. He's not around so much now that the boys are adults and we don't split their time between us. He's a friend I don't see, if that makes sense. If I needed him, he would be there and vice versa. Unless he was medieval-jousting, in which case whatever it was would have to wait until Monday.

My current husband. He has made a few appearances in the book already. I just don't want to elaborate. We are not mutually exclusive. We do, quite happily, co-exist.

My two sons. Both wonderful independent people in their own right; let's leave them that way.

My boss and store director. Nothing good or even bad enough to say.

My doctor. Might have got a mention if I had written this book ten years ago but now, every time I have an appointment, it is with a different locum and there is no way I am penning portraits of all of them.

JUNE NEWTON

Wednesday 4th August

There are books I have read and entirely forgotten. Most of them, actually. I read everything by Milan Kundera and can remember only the gynaecologist who fathered scores of local children. That I do remember. Is everything else lost, just because I can't remember it? Food passes through the body. I don't feel the benefit now of a macrobiotic yoghurt I drank in January, though, do I? But sentences, descriptions, dialogue and other moments in books? One of the receptors in my brain must have recorded them and laid them down into some kind of incremental accumulation of knowledge. I can happily watch old movies up until the point when I see the murderer. Then I'm like, 'Oh, hello. We've met before.'

The strangest picture of the afterlife just came into my head. What if it was like that experience of sitting down to watch a film and realising you've seen it before? What if it is just a replay? You can only read books you have read before. And only eat meals you ate before. And then, when you finish them, you start again. A permanent state of déjà vu, and you can't try anything new. You get wiser and wiser and more and more learned but there is nothing you can do with the knowledge. Your brain just expands in the expanding space around you.

Thursday 5th August

Talk at work today of store closure. Not official. In fact no trace of any official source that I could find whatsoever. A staffroom rumour, I think. The last document I saw, which I wasn't supposed to see, had our store as 'spared from closure'. We weren't even on the undecided list and none of those that were have yet been closed. But these rumours are unstoppable among a large staff, simply because everyone wants to be the teller and not the told.

Someone really should keep at least one of these provincial department stores open, if only as a museum. Portsmouth does very well with The Victory. People flock there to see the old ship and walk around it, but it doesn't sail anywhere anymore. Our store they could preserve. Technology-wise, it was probably last approaching state of the art in 2010. The current fashions aren't far off that date either. It would be an attraction and at least a half-day out, to visit 2010 WORLD. No need for a gift shop, either, there is nothing in the building we aren't desperately hoping someone will buy.

Career suicide. Not necessary in my line of work. It's going to happen anyway.

If you did have a career in suicide, it would be one of those jobs where only the truly useless succeed. The minute you showed any talent for it at all, you'd be dead.

Friday 6th August

Our postman will be away next week. I don't know if he is telling everyone or just me.

"Holiday," he said.

"That's nice," I said – you know, as you do. "Where are you going?"

"Poland," he said.

My face must have betrayed my surprise.

"Never been," he explained.

"No. Nor have I. With your wife?" I knew he had a wife, as he had told me before she had been ill. That was when he was last off work, maybe a year ago.

"Just me," he said. "Auschwitz. They do tours."

Wow, OK. While I would never jump to conclusions about anyone, I did wonder what the percentage breakdown of visitors to Auschwitz might be? 50% schoolchildren and 50% Neo-Nazis? I seriously hope they do not have a gift shop.

Lunch today with Tina and she would not stop asking about the book. I haven't told her anything about it. Now it fascinates her. And she is full of totally unqualified opinions. You wouldn't begin a conversation with 'Let me tell you everything I don't know about architecture,' would you? There is an inherent flaw in that proposition. But it doesn't stop Tina expounding on writing and publishing. "Is it supposed to be funny?" she asked. Not 'Is it a comedy?' or 'Is it funny?' No, she asks in a way that suggests that even if I was trying to be funny, I would fail. Or am I reading too much into this? It would be damning if she'd just read three amusing entries and one bona-fide joke and then said 'Is it supposed to be funny?' But she's not seen a word of it. I can take criticism (I hope) but I'd prefer it to come after someone has read the book!

"I don't really read," Tina continued. "I read the book reviews people write on Amazon and they are long enough. If I read four or five reviews of a book, that's it for me, I'm all read out."

Good grief, I thought. "Maybe someone should publish a book of Amazon book reviews," I said. "You might like that."

"No," Tina said, shaking her head. "I would read the reviews of a book like that but I don't think I would want to read it."

It's very hard to be annoyed with Tina. Today she is wearing a fluffy, fleecy jumper, like a cheap sweatshirt inside out. The design is a depiction of two butterflies, decorated with beads and sequins, flying around a satin and suede quilted toad. I'd like to have written 'frog' but it was a toad. As you can imagine, irony is powerless against her. As is ever the case in our short lunch meetings, Tina had the last word.

"You realise," she said, "that you will have to get someone to read it for the talking book."

I hadn't considered this.

"You know who would be perfect?" Tina said.

This wasn't really a question, as there was no gap before she told me her answer:

"Sharon Osborne."

Saturday 7th August

I saw someone today at a road crossing and thought for a minute that I knew them. There was enough about them to remind me of someone I knew, but, just as soon as I had the thought, I realised it wasn't the person I thought it was and we passed each other as strangers. The curious thing was that, with them behind me and me still walking away, I involuntarily greeted them, the person I thought it might have been, with just a little wave of my hand and a tilt of my head. I did this into the empty space ahead of me. I caught myself doing it and thought that was an odd thing to do. I have now thought about it a bit too much and my self-analysis of that air gesture is that I was so pathetically optimistic about seeing someone I knew, that I wouldn't let it go, even after I knew it was not them. Quite sad.

Sunday 8th August

I have invented a new kind of linguistical game. I maybe have also invented a new word in 'linguistical' as well, from the look of the red underline provided by my spellcheck. It's a who, how, what, where, when, why game. You take questions that work very comfortably with one or more of these words and then swap them out. Like this:

Where are you? – Simple enough, unless you are Len, and Peggy is asking.

Who are you? – Again, easy – unless you are Len.

How are you? – Fine, thanks for asking.

What are you? – Getting tougher. A woman. A writer. This is best considered as a question put to you by an alien within a couple of minutes of their landing on Earth. 'Human and not scared of you' is then the right answer.

Why are you? – PhD-level question. Probably best to ask for advice from the alien.

When are you? – My favourite. Whenever you want me!

Monday 9th August

Day off today and Pipa's parents are away, so we hid out at hers. I am actually ever so slightly older than her parents. It is quite disconcerting. I am sure they are lovely but, right now, I don't think there are two people on the planet I would less like to meet than them. There is also absolutely no chance, as I told Pipa on my arrival, of me doing anything with her in her parents' bedroom. Pipa then stuck her tongue out, which I took to be a very childish reaction to my laying down of the rules, until I saw the stud in her tongue.

"Oh, right," I said. "You did it?"

Pipa nodded. "Yep," she said. "It's a bit sore, though. And there is a problem..."

"Which is what?" I asked.

"I can't use it for... you know what... for four to six weeks."

Oh dear. Four to six weeks is longer than I have known Pipa.

"Sorry," she said. "I thought it would be fun for today. Then they told me after. No oral."

There were other things we could do and did do. I left around 2pm. Pipa's tongue would heal sometime in September. *We didn't have that long to wait.* I put that sentence in italics because it can be read two ways: *We didn't have that long to wait.* Do you see what I mean? Pipa's piercing, intended to give me pleasure, has instead punctured the very thin membrane of our implausible relationship. Today was the first day I spent with her when I felt ridiculous. Maybe a girlfriend the same age as Pipa, bent backwards over the kitchen table, would have been able to concentrate on anything other than their lover's mother's cervical screening date encircled on the calendar. Not me.

What kind of a fool I am.

Tuesday 10th August

The Guns 'n' Roses album *Chinese Democracy*. It was a very long time coming. Like it might never have happened. Is that why they called it *Chinese Democracy*? I read a news report about the Chinese and Hong Kong this morning. Hence this anachronistic thought.

Quite uncommonly for me, that was the only thought I really had today. At least, it was the only thought I had that didn't have something to do with Pipa. And it is a bit rubbish. Grrr...

Wednesday 11th August

A text from Pipa. Cancelling our plans for the weekend. *'Soz,'* she says by way of a sign-off. I get to read this on my lunch break, a full six hours before I can get home, listen to Prefab Sprout's *Steve McQueen* or the Velvet Underground's *Pale Blue Eyes* and weep for the eighteen-year-old I once was and the eighteen-year-old I have known for just a week or two. Or, much more likely, both my husband and son will be home and I shall just 'stuff it in a cup', as Lou Reed would say.

Thursday 12th August

The sense of loss. I think, and I have been thinking about this much too much, I'm afraid, that the pain associated with the loss of Pipa is not just about the sex or the secrecy or the spirit of youthful adventure... actually, stop right there – yes, it is. Those three things are more than enough for anyone to lose at one time. No wonder I am struggling. Do you think it's possible that writers, properly good ones I mean (not me), feel more pain, just because they can conjure up the words and phrases to articulate it? If this is true, then it must have been excruciating to have been Shakespeare or Mark Hollis of Talk Talk. I do hope that they also had the words to describe their joy and elation too, at least in equal measure.

Friday 13th August

The worst thing about being lonely is not being able to share it with anyone.

No messages from Pipa today. I didn't message her either, of course. Same yesterday. The last time I saw her was Monday and the most recent message from her was the Wednesday cancellation text. Len has also gone to ground. The two big stories of my recent life, that were as strange as fiction and lent this book a near novel-like quality, have now just slunk away. "Never mind me," I feel like saying (to no one). "What about my readers? Do you think they are going to settle for this?" Two weeks ago I was on the best seller list. Now I'm in the dump bin with last year's desk diaries.

You know what I would like to do? Find Becky Shackleton and, whoever she is now or whatever she has done with boyfriends or guns or building societies, have her hug me. I would curl up in a ball and she would hold me. Or I would lie with my head in her lap and she would stroke my hair and tell me everything was alright. I would do the same for her but it wouldn't be the same. I don't think I could give comfort to anyone. Maybe my sons, but that's different. I need to be comforted. I really need someone to tell me they love me.

Oh dear. Where did that Rebecca stuff come from? I'm leaving it in for now. You can't see, but it is highlighted in yellow on my laptop screen. If today throws up any genuine highlights, I am taking that passage out and replacing it.

No highlights.

Saturday 14th August

I need to stop following Pipa on Instagram. She is in London this weekend. I feel sick.

For the last time, this is not supposed to be a diary! And if it irrevocably is, then, please, not a sad one!

Pipa was too young for me. I know that sounds like the most obvious statement of all time: she was thirty-one years my junior. I don't really mean it like that. She was too young to know who Public Enemy were and that's my best ever joke: 'Flavour Flav – so good they named him one-and-a-half times.' I don't even know that she knew what *Location, Location, Location* was either: 'So good they named it thrice.' One day Pipa will read this book. I just hope her parents are not so mad about it that they won't help her with some of the references.

Sunday 15th August

I don't watch documentaries as a rule. I just think, 'What? You couldn't make something up?' And with films, I groan if I see the words 'Based on a true story'. Just lazy.

The number of times I have cried in real life versus number of times I have cried watching films must be like 5% to 95%. It is not even close. And that's not counting reading books or listening to music. Last time I cried in real life was when David Bowie died and, of course, I only knew him through his music. This imbalance must be, in part at least, down to the fact that I have lived a dull life, and one that has been, thankfully, light on tragedy. But it is also surely a sign that I truly 'live' in a fictional world. Emotion, for me, is something that exists on the screen. I cried again last night watching *The Sixth Sense* for the third time in twelve months. That part when Haley Joel Osment tells his mom that her now dead mother had seen her dancing... Toni Collette is so good in that scene.

Now I'm thinking about crying. Do we only ever cry for ourselves? I am sure this is, like, fresher's-week-level psychology, but I have never thought about it before, so maybe you haven't either? My tears weren't really for David Bowie, much as I loved him. I was crying for myself and the times in the past when, aged fourteen, I would play *Five Years* over and over again in my bedroom, feeling that life, and my part in it, was somehow deeply significant or, at least, it surely would be one day. When Bowie died I was also weeping (heavily on the street, as it happened) for myself in that moment, thinking about the fourteen-year-old me. Embarrassing admission here but, for about a year back then, I would lie in bed at night, entertaining the serious thought that I might be the second coming – you know, like the girl Jesus! Obviously, that didn't work out: amazing what a thirty-year career in retail can do for your messianic ambitions.

Monday 16th August

When my eldest son was maybe three years old, we used to play a game together in the summer called 'What can you see?' We would lie on our backs in the garden, on the decking my first husband had constructed, and look up at the blue sky above us and wait. You just fixed your eyes on the sky. You couldn't move your head to either side, as that would be cheating. And then from out of our vision, a bird would appear. Or three birds. Or, right above our noses, a bee. Sometimes, to my son's great delight, we would see an aeroplane with a vapour trail. Then clouds. And then rain. Then game over.

Now this same son has reached the age where I am double his age. The age gap between us has always been the same (like, obviously). I was twenty-four (and a bit) when I had him. But as a multiple or a fraction, we have never been closer than we are now. From twenty-four times his age to just a multiple of two. It will only get closer. He looked genuinely troubled when I told him this on Zoom, and he has a degree in mathematics.

I did once, quite wrongly, think that he might be a genius. He would have been five or six. I went into his room late one night to check he was asleep. He wasn't. He was sat up in bed in the dark and he said: "Mum, do ghosts believe in people?" I thought he was a savant! Two minutes later, I realised it was illogical and, while amusing, also pretty stupid.

My second son also delivered a classic bedtime line. He had just started school, so would have been four or five. He was crying because the other kids had picked up on his slight lisp and had teased him. I leaned over him and reassured him: "Don't be too upset. We all have things about us that we just have to deal with and make the best of in life." He looked up through his tears and said: "You mean like your big nose?"

Take note, please. That is definitely the end of any parenting anecdotes in the book!

Tuesday 17th August

I keep seeing litter in places where, if I were a litterbug, I might have dropped it myself. Same thing when driving: I see bumps and scrapes on other cars in places where, from the angle I'm looking, I could have caused it. This, I think, is the problem and limit of any scientific or philosophical theory. Humanity tries to understand the world and the universe, and the physics that govern it, but we are ourselves a product of this world. So naturally it can be made to make sense. It's all very convenient.

You look at something and you see it. Well, of course you do. That's the problem. What we need is an objective opinion.

Just reread the above paragraph. I have now officially given up on the meaning of life. It's impossible. It would be like asking Madame Bovary what she thinks of the novel.

By the way, I am refusing to go to the computer and find out whether anyone has said that before about characters in novels. I am quite sure they have. However, I would rather discuss it with a real person that doesn't know the answer than develop a relationship with the internet. It cannot be me and the internet. I may be lonely. I am lonely. But not that desperate.

Wednesday 18th August

Oh God. We have bubble tea. And bubbles of teenagers to drink it. It is not my thing. I know it isn't because, despite having an SMS text voucher for a free one when it opened, I did not try it. They could actually pay me and I wouldn't. Up to £50. And that is a lot of money for me. Yesterday my younger son declared their coffee-flavoured tea to be 'amaze'. Coffee-flavoured tea! I stood stock-still in my own lounge and I thought, 'I was born in 1971 and am forty-nine years old, have been married twice and have two grown-up children and... coffee-flavoured tea.'

I remember when Costa Coffee first opened round here. It was all wrong. Old people at the counter saying things like, 'Do you do coffee? I just want a real coffee.' These were desperate pleas for a filter coffee. What they would actually have preferred is a Nescafé or, for some of the truly aged ones, a Mellow Birds. The staff caught on soon enough and served the kids soya frappé lattes and the old people got Americanos with milk. In any of these coffee chains (outside of central London, I have to say), if you ordered an espresso, as I was wont to do, the staff always said the same thing: 'You know, it's the little one.' Every time. I worked out why, after a while. It was the cheapest coffee on the board behind the counter. So for everyone one of me, who actually wanted an espresso shot, there must have been a hundred or more old people going cheapskate-octogenarian-crazy at being handed a dribble of a drink in the bottom of a doll's-house cup. These 'you-know, it's-the-little-one' baristas had learned their lesson the hard way, many times over. For a truly cute coffee memory, I did once overhear an old man telling his adult son that he would like 'a nice cup of chino'. That will never be forgotten.

Friday 20th August

Day off and halfway through writing up the first thought (now deleted), the doorbell rang. It was Len. A tanned, healthy-looking, sunglasses-wearing Len, with a short-sleeved, striped, cotton shirt and a mint green sweater around his shoulders.

"Hello," he said. "Can we talk?"

I invited him in and suggested we sit in the garden. As we made our way down the hall, past the open doors of the lounge and the study, into the kitchen and out through the back door, Len's eyes darted about, this way and that way. He didn't actually stop and read the scribbled notes on the pad by the telephone, or take a book off the shelf and shake it out upside down until a folded note fell out, and he didn't actually open the fridge door and check the dates on the dairy goods or pull on rubber gloves and stick his hand down the bottom of the bin in the kitchen, but he might as well have done. He paid forensic attention to everything without breaking stride. I'd always wanted to meet a spy; maybe a bigamist was as close as I needed to get. A double agent indeed.

"Drink?"

"Just a water please," said Len, shifting in the garden chair so his face was shaded and he could remove his sunglasses. I went inside, took an unopened Evian from the fridge and ice from the freezer, and watched through the kitchen window as he continued his surveillance. His eyes scanned the surrounding houses, from which our neighbours might spy down on the scene below.

"So you're writing a book," Len said, as I put the tray on the table. I hadn't even sat down.

"I'm trying to," I said. "How did you know?"

"I met a friend of yours. Tina."

"Tina? How did you meet her?"

"I..." he started to say. He reset himself and began again: "There are a few things I have to say that won't come across so well. But I want you to know that it's not personal. Well, it is personal, in that I know you and like you, but, in my situation, there are things I have to do to protect my secrets."

"So you met Tina, how?"

Len came clean. "I was following you when you had lunch with her. After the lunch, I followed her and... bumped into her. It's really not so hard. You just mistake them for someone else and... you don't really need to know," he trailed off.

"No, actually I do need to know. How is it done?"

Len leaned his head back and let his eyes scan the blue of the sky. Then, no doubt having decided that I did have some rights in my own garden and that I was of course in possession of the most valuable knowledge about him, he told me how it was done.

"I said, 'Oh. Hi, Sandra.' I didn't know her name at all of course. Then when she said, 'What? I think you have the wrong person,' I said, 'Oh, I'm sorry. I thought you were someone else. You don't work in a department store then? I thought you were a friend of...' And she said, 'I know June, who works in a store.' I said, 'Really. Well that is a coincidence. I know a June. Dark hair, late forties... same?' 'Yes,' Tina said. 'How is she?' I asked and Tina, who did later tell me her name, said, 'She's writing a book.' And that is pretty much how it is done."

"And what did Tina say the book was about?"

"She said... well, it sounded a little improbable, the way she described it."

"Go on. I really want to know."

"A self-help *Fifty Shades of Grey* but funny," said Len, his eyes searching mine for any hint that this might be true.

"I haven't read the original but I imagine it is amusing enough as it is," I said.

"Probably," Len agreed. "Not my kind of thing either."

"You know I know about you," I said, thinking it was time to move this along.

"Yes," Len said. "Seeing you with Pipa was quite a surprise. I knew her family had moved here and I'd done very well to avoid them. I'd actually been trying to get Peggy to relocate since Pipa and her parents arrived on the scene. But Peggy is not one for..."

"Travelling, no," I finished his sentence.

"No."

"Peggy knows, doesn't she?"

Len breathed out and his shoulders dropped. He nodded.

"Not before the heart attack, though, but at the hospital? Your son?"

"Yes. Kind of... He's not my son. He is my other wife's son from her previous marriage. I couldn't have children. Infertile."

"And," I went on, "just briefly, if you don't mind, why did you do it?

"The two wives?"

"And two lives, yes."

"My analyst says it's emotional greed, in my case anyway."

"You have, what, like a bigamy counsellor?"

"Not specifically for that. A shrink, though, yes."

"And you tell them everything?"

Len nodded.

"Isn't bigamy illegal?"

"Doctor-patient confidentiality."

"And does your shrink know about the other shrink in another town you have been seeing?"

I must have smiled at my own joke as I said it. Len really did laugh. "I can see why your book could be funny," he said.

"There is that possibility." I was acting confident, while proceeding with caution.

"Your writing is what I wanted to discuss," said Len. "What is it about? If you don't mind me asking."

Ah, right. Why didn't I think of this? Of course the book is full of Len – his bigamy and his infamy. And even if I changed his name, changed both his names, it would still be pretty easy to work it out. I dodged Len's question: "You know there is so little chance that it is going to get published or that anyone is going to read it." As I said that, I realised it was pretty much an admission that he was in it.

"What I did," said Len, leaning forward in confessional mode, "was not great, really. That is an understatement, of course, but it was not the best way to go about things. People could have got hurt, still could, which would obviously be totally my fault."

I just let Len carry on talking.

"Peggy would be devastated if it came out. She is only putting up with it now because I am working so hard to be so charming. I was awful with her before."

"Why was that?" I asked. I really did want to know. "Why did Pipa remember you as nice and I know that you were truly horrible?"

"Analyst says split personality. Sorry to quote them again but that is what they are there for. I was two different people. I also wore different clothes, listened to different music, liked different foods."

"Wow, I can kind of understand the appeal of that."

"Plus Peggy is, you know, not the easiest to live with."

"Your long-suffered wife."

"That's good," said Len, smiling briefly. "She didn't exactly bring out the best in me."

"What about when you said you didn't want a greenhouse because of the gasses?" I had just remembered this.

"I just didn't want to spend the two grand she wanted to spend, not at that time. And I already had one."

"At your other house?"

"That's right."

I wasn't going to ask if he loved either or both of these women. I just guessed not. I am sure you can love two people, but it probably wouldn't be the motivation for marrying them both and lying to them both. Besides, what difference does it make whether he did or not?

"And you worked as a teacher before retiring, right?"

"Yes."

"And here you pretended to be in the merchant navy?"

"Yes. That was a total lie."

"So how did you have enough money coming in for both households?" This question had been around in my head for weeks now; I was glad of the chance to ask him.

"I inherited some money from my parents. They were both killed... in a fire, when I was a teenager. I'm a bigamist by the way, not an arsonist. Just in case you were thinking..."

"No! No! I was not thinking that. So you had money – enough for one life. And you worked to pay for the other one?"

"That's it."

"It's illegal and deceitful and immoral. But quite impressive nonetheless."

Len relaxed a little more into his chair. He gave me quite an adoring kind of look.

"Please don't say, 'If only I'd met you thirty years ago!'" This was me, suddenly on the defensive, thinking he might have misinterpreted my compliment.

Len smiled. "I think, honestly, I've got too many years on you. The age gap, you know." He let this last phrase hang a bit. Oh God, here we go.

"I know about Pipa," he said. "I mean, I think it's great – for you both."

"How do you know?" I asked him. "You've been avoiding us both since you saw us together."

"Instagram," Len said. "I follow her from another account just to – well, since she moved here – to keep tabs on the situation, that's all."

"I follow her on Instagram. I'm not on it, am I?"

"There was a story – that's what they call them – a while back. You were asleep in bed. She'd drawn a heart around you. In London, by the look of the other pictures. Sorry to be so prying.

I don't mean to be. It was a lovely picture."

"Well, that's all old news," I said. "I think she's moved up there now."

"Heartbroken?" Len asked, and he did mean me.

"No," I said. "My heart aches. But not for her. For me."

Len gave me a considerate look. Nice of him. Then he sat up straighter and said:

"Did she tell you she was named after an IKEA lamp?"

By the end of our garden showdown, Len and I had come to an arrangement of sorts. With regard to the book, we agreed that I would write what I wanted to write. And that, for now, I wouldn't share the writing with anyone that knew anyone else in the book. I pointedly did not promise to write him out of it. Instead we agreed to let time play its part in any difficult decisions that would have to be taken later down the line. There is, of course, the very strong possibility that I will finish the book and that is it, finito; it will never get close to being published and Len has nothing to worry about. There is also the fairly strong possibility that Len's cover will be blown by someone else before the book does or doesn't get published. Or Len or Peg or myself are hit by a bus and the only mess to clean up is that of human remains.

Len did ask to the read the manuscript. He really was keen and I do actually need a reader. I want him to read it. I desperately want to impress the hell out of him, and everyone else in the world, if I am honest. And Len, with his age, experience and humour, would be a relatively easy target for this, as compared to

Tina or Pipa or... well, I don't even know that many people, do I? Anyway, my answer was no, not yet. But it could be a yes, if he would do me one small favour.

"What's that?" Len asked, leaning in.

"Find me someone," I said. "Use your secret squirrel skills and find someone for me."

"I could do that. Who would I be looking for?"

"Rebecca Shackleton."

Saturday 21st August

Our store is officially on the amber list for potential closure. Well, that's a thing. I sat in the garden for a good half an hour, fully reclined in a lounger, watching the clouds and the birds and the sky, just as I did with my son twenty years ago. I never did think that I could change the world. Now I realise you really don't have to; the world changes anyway, whether you like it or not. Yes, the planet is spinning. It's a merry-go-round; people get on, people get off, new people get on, more people get off.

I had a dream last night but before I tell you it, I should explain that my rule with dreams is that I can only tell or be told them in a one-sentence pitch. Like in Hollywood. You know, how *Alien* was '*Jaws* in space.' Well, that would be a good dream description for me. What I don't need to hear is a seemingly endless succession of random events punctuated only by the words 'and then'. Dreams have the most awful narrative structure. One sentence and you're done is the rule in my house. My eldest son is really good at it now: "I was a wasp," he announced the other morning, "and you killed me." My dream last night, in one line: a severed head was found in a Bag For Life. Hardly what Waitrose intended. An excellent title for a thriller that I could write, though.

I'd put my name above the title. Second book = brand recognition.

JUNE NEWTON'S

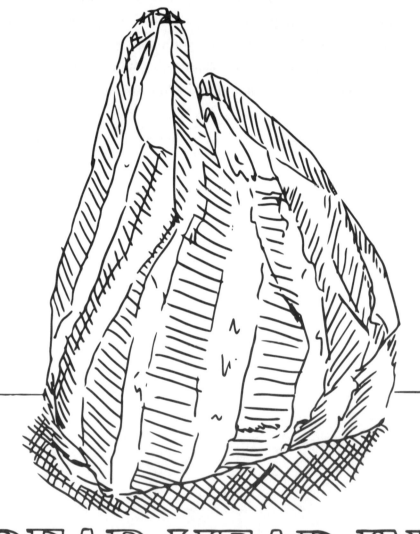

DEAD HEAD IN A BAG FOR LIFE

Nothing at all from Pipa, the IKEA lamp. It's been discontinued: the relationship and the wall-mounted spotlight I found online in the 1994 catalogue. We had the shortest time. She was over the age of consent and I was just under the age of descent. A small window of opportunity and we took it. I will not let myself feel anything other than very lucky it happened at all. Not officially anyway. The whole thing ran on teenage time, as it was. Meet one day, have sex in the woods the next, run off to London, get back home and get over it – it's finished. It doesn't mean she won't remember me; I would never ever have forgotten such a thing, if I had had even the briefest encounter with someone thirty years older than me when I was eighteen. It just means Pipa doesn't need to actually see me, call me or text me to help her remember me. I think.

If, at some point in your life, you fell into a coma, and your only experience of anything from that point on was through dreams, do you think, if you died in that coma, that you would have had less than a full life? Does it matter that the relationships, sex, meals, monsters, whatever you dreamt about, weren't real, as long as you experienced them in dream mode? I'm not at all sure. Would you even know the difference?

JUNE NEWTON

Sunday 22nd August

Once, at some point in the late nineties, my first husband's sister stayed with us for a couple of nights. She was older than him. They weren't close and I wasn't much a fan of her either. She had split up with a boyfriend and was visiting the university here with the idea of enrolling as a mature student. She was probably thirty at the time. On the morning she left, I stripped her bed to wash the sheets and found a very ample-sized vibrator under the duvet. This was not something I could do much about. And not something to disclose to her brother/my husband either. She must have realised that she had left it in the bed, but she never called round to pick it up or, indeed, ever mentioned it again. In fact, I am fairly sure she never spoke to me again at any of the weddings or Christmases we shared in the few years following. I kept the vibrator for a month or so in my underwear drawer. Then, when no contact with my sister-in-law had been established, I put it in a shoebox and threw it away. The next morning I had the day off and by about 11am had become obsessed with the idea of using it. I have no idea why, I'd not touched the thing for four weeks. Now I was rabid enough to go out to the back yard in the pouring rain and find... that the bins had already been collected. I'm not sure what the moral or lesson of this story is, other than that I suffered a profound sense of loss for something that I didn't want when I did have it. I felt much the same way after divorcing my first husband.

Monday 23rd August

Time spent writing versus time spent daydreaming about my successful life as an author of a best selling book... oh, about 50/50 at the moment.

Tuesday 24th August

Cryptocurrencies. That's the latest thing for my eldest son. He lives in Newcastle now, having graduated there. His birthday is next week so I went on to Amazon to see if I could get him a Bitcoin wallet. Yes, as I quickly realised, that was a dumb thing to be doing! Now that I know more, of how much I didn't know, about cryptocurrencies, I think I could design and sell some actual Bitcoin wallets. There must be other mothers as clueless as me. Come Christmas, I could be rich – in real money.

I'm old, I think. It still freaks me out now when I transfer money to my sons from my phone. When pocket money first went cashless, and the banking app asked for a reference, I would write 'cigarettes', 'alcopops' or sometimes 'flowers for your mother'. I never saw any evidence of any purchases, certainly not any flowers for me. The banks should make pocket money traceable. It can't be that hard to do. Now that I am a little more up to speed on Bitcoin, I know they could use a blockchain. It would be a great innovation for grandparents who hand out £25 in birthday money to see where it ends up. They want to see it spent on jigsaw puzzles and books, though, don't they? Not skunk.

Wednesday 25th August

"Are you worried?" Winona asked.

I was about to cash up the till for the day. She was leant over the counter from the sales floor side, far more casually than a customer ever would.

"About?" I asked.

She was chewing gum. "Life?" she said, with the same slightly angle-askew look that I thought I remembered from *Reality Bites*.

I carried on with my counting and totalling. Winona was a great one for doing impulsive things but I liked her best as a listener. She was a brilliant listener.

"I think that nothing I really worry about ever turns out as bad as thought it would," I said.

Winona brought her gum forward between her teeth. "Uh-huh," she said, keen to hear more.

"Most bad things that happened to me just happened so suddenly that there was no time to worry about them," I continued. "I fell off a wall in Holland about seven years ago, went into a coma and spent a week in a Dutch hospital. That was awful but I wasn't expecting it, so, you know, at least I didn't have to beat myself up about it for months in advance."

"Right," she said.

"Imagine how bad it would be if someone told you you would

be fighting for your life in a coma exactly eight weeks from now."

Winona's eyes widened as she considered this.

"The worry would cripple you," I said. "Be grateful of great misfortune, is what I say."

She nodded slowly, appearing to agree.

"Now, if I lose my car keys and wallet on the same day – well, that's two less things that I *didn't* have to worry about!"

"I like that," said Winona with a big smile.

"Like with horoscopes," I said. "Best to read them at the end of the day, just to check whether they got it right. Reading them in the morning is way too stressful."

"Are you a superstitious person?" Winona asked. This is what it is like taking to her – she always had me talking about myself.

I shrugged. "A little bit about magpies. I like to see two together. Just one is a bad omen."

"What do you do if you see one?" Winona asked.

"I salute the lone ones three times," I said, "to break the curse."

Winona stood up and saluted three times.

"I'm not sure you are supposed to do that indoors," I said.

"Isn't that umbrellas?" Winona correctly queried.

"Yeah. Good point. Anyway, my sympathy is really with the magpie. They obviously like hanging about in pairs."

"They do," Winona agreed.

"It's not so much the bad luck, more the loneliness of the solo magpie that frowns me down."

"That does what?" Winona asked. "Frowns you down?"

I had finished with the cashing up so she followed me through to the backroom office where the safe was. There was no one else around.

"What's 'frowns you down'?" she asked again.

I sat on a desk and explained. "It's a phrase I made up," I said. "Like 'awesumnal'."

Winona looked confused.

"For something awesome that happens in autumn," I said.

"Like the leaves?"

"Yes and acorns and..." I couldn't actually think of any more.

"Halloween?" Winona suggested, trying to help me.

"That's its own thing. Maybe this is why 'awesumnal' never caught on," I laughed.

"When you make up your next word maybe don't go seasonal," Winona said. "You'd have more chance if you could use it all year round."

"You're right," I admitted.

"And you know we don't say 'autumn', we call it 'fall'?"

I hadn't even thought of that.

"Awe-fall. So really you have reinvented the word 'awful'," she said. "Which is not what you meant at all."

I was a little deflated.

"But I love 'frowns me down'," she said, and gave a little skip. We are almost exactly the same age but I don't do hops and jumps when excited. I wish I did but... I wasn't likely to start now. "How can I use it?" Winona asked.

I couldn't really say what would frown Winona down, it would be something personal to her. For me though, when I am walking alone through town and pass other people in conversation together, that frowns me down. It deeply saddens me, actually. Walking at dusk past warmly-lit restaurant and pub windows, with tables of people chatting and laughing together, just kills me. It is irrational; I am probably just as often one of the people talking with someone when a lone person walks past. And the times when I am in groups of people in a pub, I am often bored and desperate to leave. But still it gets to me. I think if I could actually hear the conversations, I'd be less despondent. But when I can't hear, I seem to just imagine that, whatever they are saying is fascinating and revealing and, I don't know, somehow life-enhancing. And if it is raining as well, when I peer in these cosy windows, honestly, I would need Charles Dickens to describe my own misery.

I explained all that to Winona. "Well, you can always talk to me," she said. "Whenever the world frowns you down, you can talk to me and I will smile you up."

I tried a smile.

"That's not so good is it?" Winona said.

I shook my head: "Doesn't rhyme."

Thursday 26th August

I went to a bookshop to check out the competition. A proper one: Waterstones. Big mistake. I was scared of the blockbusters, stacked high on the tables out front. But I was even more terrified by the single copy novels that surely never sell. And there are so many of them. I could write all of this and my book could be one of them. And that's if I even get published! The real winners seem to be the graphic designers and illustrators – they get paid whether anyone reads the book or not.

I am aiming to think and write with more clarity, precision and truth until I get to something as truly great as Snoopy's *"I think I'm allergic to mornings."* Admittedly, I have a long way to go. The closest I have got so far is *"Drowning is a fate worse than death."* And I can't really see that on a coffee mug.

Two more recent attempts:

Life begins ten years before you turn fifty.

My favourite word? Incomparable. Really, no competition.

Friday 27th August

Nothing happens here! Is that fair comment? Am I just lacking imagination? I should have just sat down and written myself a novel – a fantastical one of wizards and dragons. My mistake was to base the book on myself. Bigamy and same-sex sex are news. June goes to work is not. How did I ever let Pipa and Len go? They weren't just people, like everyone else round here, they were characters. That phrase – 'like they stepped out of a novel' – well, they have stepped out of mine!

Saturday 28th August

I am very trusting of people. I trust them to do whatever they are going to do. When my sons were in their teens, I trusted them to drink, do drugs, have sex, fail at things, excel and succeed at others. They didn't let me down. Now I trust that Pipa will just go and get on with her life. I'm sure she won't disappoint. Unfortunately, I have less trust in me. Believe in yourself, the self-help books say. Well, I have been reading and re-reading these pages and can honestly say that I have more belief in the June Newton as she is written than the June Newton that is doing the writing. Is that progress? Or am I now fully delusional?

Monday 30th August

Len has sent a text. He has news on Rebecca. He thinks he has found her. I called him straight away.

"That's amazing. Where is she?"

"London," Len said. "But there is something I don't think you know. You might be surprised."

"What?"

"Maybe we should meet. It might be better if I am with you

when I tell you."

"I... I can't. What is it? I can't bear waiting to hear anything bad. Just tell me."

"OK. I'll tell you and then I'll come round. I'll be at yours in ten minutes."

"What is it?"

"She's taken your name."

"She's...?"

"She is June Newton. Has been since 1998, as far as I can tell. I'm coming round now. Stay there. I'll show you what I found."

"Rebecca is June Newton?"

"I'm coming. Hang up. I'm coming."

I hung up. Wow. I didn't expect that. It was so astounding. I couldn't even have unexpected it. What on earth?

Len duly sped round and showed me everything he had found out about Rebecca Shackleton/June Newton. She lived in an apartment in Marylebone. She was wealthy enough to own the flat (at least £2 million, Len estimated) without appearing to have a mortgage. She may have other property but public records of her finances and business activities were patchy, at best. She had adopted my date of birth too and used it interchangeably with her own. She was not married. She did not appear to have been married and was very likely single. And she looked, as Len put it, "like a real stunner." He had seen her on two separate occasions on Marylebone High Street, where she lived. There were no police records on June Newton. However a Rebecca Shackleton was on record as missing in suspicious circumstances, circa 1994. There was more. A lot more. There were details of what she had for lunch, for goodness' sake. But all of it paled into insignificance in the light of the BIG FACT: she had taken my name!

Tuesday 31st August

Do not expect me to have any sparklingly original ideas or wryly-observed thoughts today, please. Having a proper identity crisis that is not mental but FACTUAL.

Wednesday 1st September

Bloody hell! Now I have something else to think about. Our store is on the red list. It was only ten days ago we were on amber. Now they are talking about closure in October. The news will be announced to the press today. An all-store clearance sale will start on Monday. Oh, and management are looking for people to talk to the local TV reporters this afternoon. Peggy and I have been nominated as the two longest-serving members of staff. If I do it I will have to drive home at lunchtime and pick up the T-shirt. I promised myself – and you all – that I would wear the three wolves howling at the moon shirt when the moment came. And now here it is, with absolutely no notice. There are tears in the staff room – strangely, from some of the younger girls who have only worked here a year at best. All the talk is about redundancy pay. Three weeks for every year of service. "Hello," I thought, "that's over a year's pay for me." No wonder it was the newbies who were crying. I'm in a pretty good mood, scribbling down these notes on my morning break. Besides, this book now has a narrative arc to add to the bigamy subplot, steamy intergenerational lesbian love affair and identity fraud. Not bad at all! None of this was planned. None of this, save for the store closure (predictable in hindsight), could I ever have hoped to have made up.

OK, so I have been home and back and I have the T-shirt. I'm not wearing it yet, just in case our otherwise anonymous store director materialises, *Star Trek*-style, on the deck of the Ladies' Fashions and stops me from wearing it on the TV. I'll slip it on at the last minute and then it will be too late for anyone to stop me. It can't possibly be a dismissible offence, can it? I do have that redundancy windfall to consider. 6.45pm is when the cameras roll. It is 5pm now. This is agonising. I can't even share my butterflies with Peggy; her friend on the second floor says she's gone out to "fix herself up."

Everyone is asking what I am going to say. I hadn't thought about it. What *am* I going to say? Don't I just have to answer their questions? I'm not doing a desk piece. I don't have to segue into Dominic with the weather. I mean, C'mon, don't make me any more nervous.

We are in front of the cameras now, standing outside the main store entrance with what must be thirty or forty people looking on. Everyone is staring at my T-shirt. Of course they are! Our store director looks a little freaked by it, but I am sure I can lip-read the producer saying, "Love it. Keep it." Peggy is zipped-up in a waterproof jacket and rocking from one foot to the other. She is either nervous or cold; it is a bit nippy. Either way, it is not quite the glamorous look I was expecting from Peggy.

"OK. Quiet please." That's the producer to everyone in earshot. "And cameras!" he says, loudly. "Rolling," replies the cameraman. Roving reporter, Bruce Handsome, who I would recognise from a hundred metres, is now standing just a few feet from Peggy and I. That's not his real name, by the way, just what I have always called him. Bruce is listening for the cue from the studio and he gets it:

"Indeed Gary, I am here now with June Newton and Peggy Hutchins, the two longest-serving staff members and, oh, wow, that is some shirt Peggy."

Peggy! What?! He thinks I'm Peggy. That's what flashed through through my mind. I started to say something and then just ate a mouthful of air. Peggy had unzipped and discarded her jacket. She was wearing... I can barely describe this now! She was wearing an oversize T-shirt with black, block-capital letters saying: FRANKIE SAYS... SAVE OUR STORE.

"Frankie said relax," said Peggy, directly into the camera. "That was 1984. Now Frankie says, stand up and fight!"

OMFG. She's rehearsed! And the camera crew loves her.

"How old are you Peggy?" she is asked.

"I'm sixty-four!" she replied, like she was telling everyone she was 101. Fuck!

I was asked a question and I did my bit about our customers having 'in-disposable incomes'. Stupid thing to say; too clever by half, and it went right over Bruce's pretty head. The whole thing was over so soon. Peggy was mobbed. I was left standing alone with our store director. "Interesting shirt," he said, eyes fixed on the three wolves howling at the moon. "Let's not wear that tomorrow."

I knew exactly how it had gone down when my youngest son texted me: "Did you see? Peggy was on the telly!"

Friday 5th November

Hello again. See the date above. Big jump in the timeline. A lot has happened. So much has changed. For you, though, it is a mere turn of the page. September to November, in a flip. For me, well, you are about to find out.

Just to be clear, I had no intention of writing a novel until I started living in one! And the fact that I am the central character is, of course, unavoidable. What you have in your hands is a book that was meant to be a fairly uncommon form of literature, a journal of thoughts and ideas that became, for convenience more than any other reason, a diary of sorts. Then my life (my suddenly surreal life) rather hijacked the whole project and left me no choice but to write it up and put it all in. I have done my best to keep the first part more or less as it was intended. Then, as you know, all of a sudden, it's the greatest story ever told! Sorry about that.

Saturday 6th November

An extremely rare event for me today. I bought a single train ticket. In fact, now that I am thinking about it, I may never have done that before. I can't remember going anywhere and not coming back. Annoyingly, it was no cheaper than a return, but that is a tiny speck of a detail compared to the seismic magnitude and mega-symbolic significance of the fact that I moved to London!

Even better, I am sitting back at my window on Wardour Street. Typing 'I moved to London' is just as great as doing it. I live on the page now.

Sunday 7th November

I sense that some of you might want some detail on the circumstances of my departure. There may be some of you that care about regional department stores and retail in general. There are doubtless others who are thinking about the house and husband and sons I left behind. I love my sons, don't get me wrong, but I think the best thing I can teach them, at their advanced ages of twenty-two and twenty, is that their mother has a life of her own.

I'm all about the what-happens-next, both in this book and in my life; they are pretty much the same thing now, after all. So please allow me to arrange the few things I brought with me in my room, charge the laptop, and reacquaint myself with what Bruno's has to offer by way of fried meals and toasted snacks. I have major plans and a target for next week. Namely, Rebecca Shackleton.

Wednesday 10th November

Rebecca (the other June Newton) lives in Marylebone on the

corner of Marylebone High Street and Moxon Street. According to Len, she pops out every morning and goes over the road to Pret A Manger for a coffee, a green juice and a salad. Len's notes are way too much information but you don't want to complain when someone does a job too well, do you? Actually, when I first went back to work after having the boys, my first husband and I had a cleaner. She came once a week for about a year, until she went on holiday and a friend of hers filled in for a fortnight. This interim cleaner was a revelation. She didn't just origami the end of the toilet paper roll into a pointed triangle, she attacked the grouting in the bathroom with an old toothbrush and scrubbed the mildew off the shower curtain. When our regular cleaner returned, I left her a note saying thank you for sending us such an excellent stand-in, adding, 'She was fabulous.' Well, I came home to a note from our cleaner telling me just how unhappy she was with her friend; how she was going to tell her they were finished; that was the last time she would give her an opportunity like that; how she didn't need to come on like Mary Poppins; using her obvious OCD to get her (my cleaner) fired! I can only paraphrase now as I did try to keep the note, but the following week I found it missing from the pinboard in the kitchen, one of the few things my cleaner ever actually tidied away. The point of all this being, I guess you *can* complain about someone doing a job too well.

I'm aware that I am killing time here, avoiding writing about Rebecca. This is because I want to get it right.

On Monday I lurked about on Marylebone High Street all morning and half the afternoon and I did not see Rebecca. I saw a lot of very confident, wealthy and well-to-do women, which was fascinating at first and then more than a little depressing. It was possible, I thought, that Rebecca had been away for a long weekend. I went back to Bruno's and the Soho flat and returned yesterday to do it all over again. Same time, same place, but this time, as I completed the small circuit I had walked around and around the day before, there she suddenly was, twenty yards in front of me. I only narrowly avoided her seeing me, by diving into a shop. I watched as she emerged from the Pret and strode back to her flat. Embarrassingly, that's all I did yesterday: I looked at her. And I looked at her in awe. This was a complete failure on my part and not at all the plan, but, the second I saw her, I knew it wasn't right. I wasn't right. There was a huge gulf in class and I seriously needed to up my wardrobe. Rebecca stepped out to get coffee in ankle boots with a bit of a heel, tight black leather jeans, khaki cotton scoop neck T-shirt top, black leather jacket and a charcoal grey scarf. Her chest was partly exposed; the flash of flesh in November was clearly a key part of the total look. Her hair was long, perfectly 'unstyled' and equally perfectly highlighted. It wasn't just me looking at her, I noticed. Two drivers, both male, were particularly keen to slow down and stop for no reason other than to watch her cross the road in front of them. In contrast and, even though I wasn't wearing one of my drab work suits that could have covered MFI sofas in the eighties, I was wearing navy wool trousers from Next, black leather flats from Schuh, an old George at Asda blouse, a metallic weave cardigan from, of all places, Matalan. I had topped it all off with a waterproof jacket from, oh, idontknowwhere.com. I did have the Balenciaga belt but that must have been crying out for help 'I belong here – this woman doesn't!'

I had more clothes at the flat at Wardour Street but they were no better than today's outfit, they were worse. Rebecca and I were the same age but you wouldn't know it to look at us. Maybe naked we'd have similar bodies but I didn't have a plan to sidle up to her in a sauna. Her clothes took five years off her and mine added five to me. A ten-year wide chasm had opened up between us.

My hair was also crying out – drying out – to be fixed up. That could be dealt with. The smart move was to book a cut and blow dry in Marylebone. Rebecca appeared today around 11.40am, which was consistent with the Len schedule. That would mean a 9am appointment would work. So I booked in at a salon round the corner. Very swanky but £95 for a haircut! What the hell, this was an emergency. For the clothes, I thought I'd walk back to Soho via Bond Street. But I'm by no means a Londoner yet. Six nights in a year doesn't grant you resident status or much of a grasp of where anything is. I headed off in what turned out to be the opposite direction. I stopped a few streets away to consult my phone and found myself standing opposite a Designer Exchange. How perfect, I thought. This was the answer. I felt so clever; all these clothes were previously owned and were not only cheaper than the real deal but had a history to them that I could make my own.

Inside, the shop was small and dark and the rails were stuffed with clothes. I kept the image of Rebecca in my mind and avoided anything too colourful. I picked out a very worn-round-the-edges Gucci handbag. £150. That definitely gave the impression I had owned it for years. The size 10 Alexander McQueen zipped biker dress would have fitted me but it was £1,500 and suggested a Tarantino-style standoff, in which Rebecca and I played two rival underworld assassins. The problem with that scenario was that Rebecca might well actually be an underworld assassin, and I knew that I wasn't. I picked up a Missoni top for £40, deep green and with the same neckline as Rebecca had worn today. The claret Stella McCartney single button blazer was an easy call at £70. The weather was forecast for twelve degrees and no rain: I could get away without buying a coat. The Isabel Marant grey wool trousers were perfect at £160 but had the weirdest lace ties around the ankles, like a tramp or a scarecrow would have. I wasn't previously aware of this fashion trend, I have to say. And what if Rebecca made a boho hobo joke? That would be too much. So I asked, very kindly, if they would cut the ties off – after I had paid for them, of course. I splashed out £250 on a pair of Chanel quilted ankle boots. They were my size. As the sales guy said, probably for the thousandth time, "In this shop, every shoe that fits is a Cinderella moment." Then I spotted a McQueen biker jacket. It was wool rather than leather but had all the zips in all the right places. It was way cooler than the blazer and had the benefit of keeping me warm. Worth an extra £90, I thought, as I put the Stella McCartney back. All in, we were looking at £630.

"I want to wear it all now," I said, as I searched my purse for the credit card. "I don't suppose you want my clothes?" The assistant shook his head as the payment went through. "There's an Oxfam back on the High Street," he said, before adding, "Keep the belt. Very nice."

He was by no means the fancy dress shopkeeper in Mr Ben, but I really did walk out of that store into a new and now seemingly fictional world. I was transformed, on the outside and the inside. I don't know if you have ever walked down the street thinking you were in a film. That's how I felt just then. I didn't start it, I want you to know; the people who were looking at me started it! I've never had that feeling before. The sense that I was being watched. It was a first for me. I walked past a restaurant and people looked up, both men and women. I sat in a café and the people coming in checked me out. This, I can well imagine, is a delusion of glamour, one step away from mental illness, but, for me, you have to understand, it was all so new and other-worldly that I could only imagine it as a film I was in. I was a long way from thinking that this could be my life but I could play the part.

Back in Soho this evening. Claudio served me egg and chips in Bruno's. Then I tried to sleep. What could I possibly dream, I wondered, that could be any more like a dream than tomorrow?

The next morning I was early at the salon. I didn't know it but I had already seen my stylist smoking on the street around the corner. He, who would later introduce himself as Brian, came in just after me. "Oh, hello!" he said, in a thick Glaswegian accent. "You are new." Only his 'hello' was more like 'helloooo' and 'new' was 'noooooo'.

"I'm Brian," he continued, "You know, it's the boys name for Bryony!"

I liked him a lot. I liked the place a lot. I could get used to a scalp massage at nine in the morning. And I readily accepted the free-flowing frothy cappuccinos with enough foam to cover my upper lip.

"Leave it on for a hot one," Brian said. "There's Veet in the coffee."

"Veet?" I asked.

"Hair remover, dear!" He pulled a tube from a tray beside him. "I know it's November but Movember is supposed to be for guys!"

I looked up at him – at us both in the mirror – me with a white moustache.

"Don't worry. JK!" he chimed.

I had no idea what he was talking about.

"I use it down there on my..." He pointed down at his low-slung cargo shorts.

"Legs?" I guessed, in all naivety.

Brian loved this: "Sorry, which part of Squaresville did you say you were from?"

I have now, in writing this up later, only just realised that 'hot one' was short for 'a hot minute' and 'JK' was 'joking'. Honestly, nine-and-a-half out of ten of my Google searches lead me to the pages of the Urban Dictionary. In the summer I had actually thought about buying an Urban Dictionary from Amazon. I stopped myself when I thought there probably is a word in it for forty-nine-year-olds that buy printed versions of online resources: 'Saddos' or 'Dix' or something cleverer than that.

Brian had a Nicorette patch on his arm and another one showing through the string vest he was wearing.

"Oh that," he said, when he saw me looking. "It's been there a week. It's grafted on. I'm too chicken to rip it off. My chest stubble will grow through it. Like Chinese bamboo torture." He laughed, very loudly, at this. It was so much fun. And, as expensive and chic as it was, it was also disarmingly similar to every hair salon I have ever been in. You know, questions from the stylist about what I do for work, about husbands and kids, holidays and weekend plans. I once had an idea for Aircuts. They'd be cheaper than haircuts with the 'H' on the front, because, for the duration of an Aircut, the stylist would use their fingers as scissors. Nothing would actually get cut, but you could go every day and enjoy the inane chit-chat. Brian was a master of inanity; truly a level up from anything I had experienced before. I was there on a Wednesday and quite early on in the appointment, he asked, "Heavy weekend or just chill?" I'd had quite an eventful start to the week so I was hard pressed to even remember Saturday or Sunday. Minutes later he asked for my plans for the weekend, meaning the one that was three days away. I had a hard job answering that one too. Then came holidays and, as it was indeed November, the question, 'Going anywhere nice this year?' was only equalled in unanswerability by its twin enquiry, coming seconds later: "Been anywhere nice this year?" But much better than all of these questions (and female facial hair remedies) was that my hair looked fabulous. And I hadn't even thought about Rebecca, let alone had a panic attack. That was still to come. I walked out of the door an hour later and £120 lighter. I gave a £20 tip to Brian, after he, very openly, dropped the Veet cream into my Gucci bag.

The next hour was nerve-racking. It was beyond that, really, it was agony. A horribly long wait for something I could not even guess at how it would turn out. I spent most of the time in the Oxfam on the High Street where, just yesterday, I had dropped off my country-mouse clothes. They had a book section and it was small enough not to be daunting, unlike the aptly-named Daunt Books just up the road. I wasn't reading the books, I was taking them off the shelves to see how many pages they had and then counting the words on a line and lines on a page in order to, with the help of the calculator on my phone, produce an approximate word count. This was a pretty good 'taking my mind off it' activity and, surprisingly, not that depressing: Evelyn Waugh's *Decline and Fall* had 50,000 words (I had read that in A-Level English); a Douglas Adams sequel to *Hitchhiker's Guide To The Galaxy* was less; *Bridget Jones's Diary* was, admittedly, close to 80,000 but *Generation X*, the Douglas Coupland book, was way back down at 48,000, and still described on the front as "a groundbreaking novel." It was also a book I had loved thirty years ago and, as I didn't have a copy in London (I didn't have any books or any things in London), I bought it to pay for the time I had spent loitering. Then I went looking for a loo.

And then.

And then I saw Rebecca again. She was on the march back to her flat with her Pret coffee in one hand and lunch in a bag in the other. She cut across the traffic that had again come to its slack-jawed, open-mouthed halt. I doubt she even knew what a zebra crossing was. She was dressed in more or less the same outfit as the day before. But in a change to the routine, not at all predicted by Len's notes, she had come out on today's lunch run a good forty minutes early. This time I didn't have a chance to dash and hide, which is what I would have done if hadn't been caught between her and her doorway and frozen to the spot. I didn't move. And then, as she got to within five yards of me and as her eyes met mine, I said, "Rebecca."

And everything stopped. Time stopped. Like when you jump to the end of the movie on Amazon Prime and the wheel spins for just a second as the data buffers and the film starts up again.

"June," Rebecca said, surprised.

"June," I said back to her. That was her name too, after all, and had been for twenty years or more.

"Yes," she said and just stared at me. "Sorry about that."

I was staring at her too. She had lost the mole on her cheek. I stared her down. Now it was Rebecca who looked like she was going to make a run for it. But I guess she also knew that I must know she lived here, as I was standing outside her door. She stood her ground. "Are you..." she paused to think, "just in town for the day?"

"No." I shook my head as I said it. That can add weight to a 'no', I think. "I'm staying in Soho... for the foreseeable."

I looked at Rebecca. She was continuing to calculate, like someone doing sums in their head.

"Ah," Rebecca said, turning the key in the lock. "OK". She was looking at my outfit in what seemed like complete amazement. "You'd better come in then."

The front door opened onto a small hallway and a set of stairs that climbed above the shop below. The door on the first floor opened with Rebecca's thumbprint and was, I saw as I walked through it, made of about four inches of thick metal. Inside, it was too dark to see anything until Rebecca adjusted the dimmer control and the room faded up into vision, like the opening scene of a serious play. This all felt like a very serious play; one by Harold Pinter, if I had to make a guess. The apartment was impressive – in its oppressiveness. An open-plan kitchen that was all black marble and steel. Nothing out on the surfaces other than a pack of cigarettes and an ashtray. There were three large sofas, low to the ground and in leather so black they were shapeless like the ghostly monster in *Spirited Away*. No television or screen that I could see but a very large framed photograph that I actually recognised as the Avedon portrait of Nastassja Kinski with the snake.

"Richard Avedon," I said. Rebecca just stared at me. She hadn't spoken a word since we came in off the street. She put her

Pret purchases down on the vast, stained-black, wooden desk in the middle of the room. She didn't take her eyes off me as she sat down behind the desk. She didn't invite me to sit either.

"OK," she said. "The jacket. Where did you get it?"

That was not the kind of question I was expecting. And it wasn't asked in a friendly way either, like one woman might say to another, "Oh, that is nice. Where did you get that?" It wasn't like that at all. It was a threatening question. Menacing. This wasn't going well.

"It's McQueen," Rebecca said, answering for me. Then she saw my boots. "Chanel?"

How the hell can she tell that? That's what I thought, not that I had that much time to think.

"June," Rebecca said, "I want you to put the Gucci bag on the table." My hand tightened on the bag straps. "Put it on the table!" she commanded. I put it on the table. "Push it over to me." I pushed the bag across the desk to within her reach. "Now take a step back," Rebecca said. I stepped back.

"Right. So now," Rebecca said – and I thought I could detect a light tremble in her voice, "you are going to tell me..." (I was really scared, suspended in this mid-sentence.) "...Tell me why are you wearing my clothes?"

Why was I what?! I didn't say that, I thought it. I didn't say anything immediately. What the hell?! What?! All my lines I had rehearsed last night about the jacket, you know, like it "having all the zips in all the right places," and the bag, "Oh this old thing? Yeah, I just can't bear to let it go. So many memories." All of that was out the window. And the question I was faced with – that had been put to me – that question, just so we all understand it, was...

"Why are you wearing my clothes!?" That was Rebecca again, trying the 'SAY THE SAME THING AGAIN BUT LOUDER' trick that had made me put the bag on the table.

"I bought them yesterday," I said. "I only bought them yesterday."

"Where?" she asked. "Where did you get them?"

"A designer exchange," I said.

"On Blandford Street."

I nodded. "Yes."

The look on Rebecca's face changed while I was looking at her, as one big thought crossed her mind. I could see it come over her. Like a field moving from shade to sunlight as a fast cloud passed by.

"Unbelievable. Impossible," Rebecca said. "I sold them those clothes. I thought they were too good for a charity shop. So I sold the clothes to them." Rebecca paused before completing the picture: "And you...you went there and bought them. And you didn't know they were my clothes?"

"No," I said. "Are they...*all* your clothes?"

Rebecca stood up again now and looked at me. "The jacket and boots, for sure. The top probably was mine. I had so many like that. The trousers... I had a similar pair with these stupid ties around the ankles. I never wore them."

"I cut them off."

"Fuck me," Rebecca said, looking intently at the bottom of my trousers. "You did too."

"And the bag?" I asked.

"Let me show you something about this bag," Rebecca said. She turned it on its side, careful so as not to throw all my things across the desk. She felt with her fingers along the seam on the underside, and then stopped. "Hold on, I need tweezers."

She made to go off on in search of some.

"You can sit down," she said, as she walked into the darkness at the end of the hallway. So generous. I pulled a chair out opposite hers. Remember she stole your name, I said to myself. She's the one with the questions to answer, not me. Not me, who just accidentally happened to turn up in her entire last season's wardrobe. She's the criminal with the thumb-unlocking bank-vault-style, solid metal front door...

Rebecca returned and used the tweezers to prise a small white envelope from out of the bag's hidden seam.

"They paid me a hundred quid for this bag and I gave them two wraps of coke. There's another one in there somewhere. Shall I get it or do you want to keep it?"

"Please take it out," I said, a little too nervously. I hadn't had any experience with drugs. Not since, aged seventeen, I took a few drags on a spliff in the one and only squat I had ever visited. I had been sick to the point of very nearly drowning in it and then woke up in a bedroom splattered with even more my own vomit and could just about make out that a boy, who I vaguely knew, who wanted to be an actor, was trying to hang himself – to death – with a neck tie from the light fixture in the ceiling.

"I'm not really a drugs fan," I said. Why did I say it like that?! My nan used to use that expression. "I'm not a fan of sprouts," she would say. "You know I'm not a broccoli fan." Thankfully, Rebecca didn't pick up on it.

"Well, that's good," said Rebecca, extracting the second packet from the bottom of the bag. I wasn't sure if she meant good for me or good for her, meaning not having to share the gear. 'Gear' was better, a more appropriate vocabulary choice – only I didn't say the word, I just thought it.

"Are all the clothes in that shop yours?" I asked. It seemed a reasonable question to me. But not to Rebecca:

"Oh fuck off. No way. Have you seen some of the shit they've got in there?"

I could only shrug.

"When I sold those – about a year ago – they tried to get me to take exchange, you know, instead of cash. Oh my God, there was this purple fucking blazer."

"It's still there," I said.

"Is it? Well, I am not surprised. Hideous."

"So, out of all the clothes in the shop I could have bought..."

"You only bought mine," said Rebecca. "That's what's so mental. We have more in common than you'd think."

"Like our names," I said.

"Ah, yes. Did I already say sorry for that?"

At this point there was a thud from above the kitchen. I looked up and there was a mezzanine level I hadn't noticed before. Everything was so ridiculously black, it was hard to make it out.

But, as I looked past Rebecca, over her shoulder, I saw a black staircase to the side of the kitchen and onto the top step a pair of feet appeared, then legs and then a full-frontal male nude lower half. My widening eyes must have painted the picture, as, without turning round, Rebecca called out: "Lucio, put some clothes on."

Rebecca smiled. "I forgot he was here," she said to me. Lucio's lower half turned and climbed back up the stairs. Nice bum. I never saw his face.

Rebecca turned and called out after him: "I think today you could go back to your dad's, OK?"

"You share custody?" I said, when Rebecca turned back to me.

"Ha. No! Although it feels like it sometimes. No, he's not my son. His father is... someone I know. Businesswise."

Lucio didn't reappear. Rebecca appeared to be wondering what to do with me, with this situation.

"So you're in town," she said. "Living here?"

"Yes."

"You know I have made a bit of money."

I looked around again at the apartment. "It seems like it," I said.

"But that's not why you are here?" Rebecca asked.

"No!"

"OK," said Rebecca, still sounding a little to me like she questioned my motives.

"I don't want your money," I said.

Rebecca looked squarely at me. "Well, I don't want you wearing my clothes. It's too much..." She trailed off.

I didn't really know how to resolve this one either. "I'll go and buy some – of my own."

"Yes," Rebecca said, "but..." She opened a drawer beside her and took out a black American Express card. "You can use this card. I feel I owe you that." She pushed the card over to me. "It's in your name, anyway." I looked at the card. It was completely smooth. No raised numbers on the front. Just gold text. It was also twice as thick as any card I had ever seen and was edged in silver. I picked it up, cold metal and heavy in my hand. I read my name, JUNE NEWTON.

"I know," said Rebecca, watching me turn it over, "You can't slip a lock with that. I guess they think people who can afford them don't need to break into houses."

I just nodded. These were not thoughts that would have come into my head.

"You can use it, though. Buy some proper clothes with it."

"Oh, no. I couldn't do that. Sorry," I said.

"Yes, you can," Rebecca insisted. "Go to Harrods, though, they know me too well in Selfridges."

She didn't wait for me to say no again.

"And please don't come out of there having spent less than ten grand."

"Ten thousand... Pounds."

Rebecca continued, "I know it sounds like a lot of money but it won't go far in there. And I'm guessing you need earrings too..." She said all this while looking me up and down for the third time. "And a manicure. And a facial. And a watch. Make it fifteen."

"Fifteen?" I said. "Thousand?" This was not so much a question as a fact check.

"I'd rather you spent twenty and didn't have to go back next week," Rebecca said. "They sell stuff out of season for the St. Barts crew – so buy yourself some summer stuff too. They'll get you a car back to…"

"Soho."

"Yes." Rebecca continued, warming to her task, "Ask them to run your card through first for 20k, then you can relax and enjoy the shopping. They'll refund anything you don't spend."

I was impressed, not by Rebecca now, but by the Harrods staff; thirty years I'd worked on the fashion floor and no one had ever asked me to do that. The most I was ever asked to hold on to was an umbrella.

"You should go. The PIN is 1207. I don't think you'll forget it." Rebecca waited for me to recognise my date of birth. It didn't take long. "I've got some loose ends to tie up." She motioned toward the mezzanine. "And work to do. But let's have dinner, yeah?"

"Tonight?" I asked. A lot had happened since we'd met on the street but we hadn't actually discussed anything yet.

"That's what I meant," she said. "Tonight."

"I'll give you back the card."

"Yes. Where do you want to go?"

I was going to say that it's not my town and… "AMA," I said, surprising us both.

"Wow. How much money do you think I've got?"

"Sorry," I quickly replied. "I'll just get less clothes."

"I'm joking. Just wasn't expecting you to say AMA, that's all. But it's perfect. Very good choice. Let's do seven. An early one. We have a lot to talk about."

Oh, yes, I thought, we really do.

"Can I use the bathroom?" I asked. I was desperate now.

"Oh, sorry, yes. It's on the right, down the hall."

I got up and picked up the Gucci bag. Rebecca eyed it a little suspiciously.

"Don't worry, the drugs are on the table," I said as I walked toward the bathroom.

"I wasn't thinking that," Rebecca called after me. "It's just... June..." I stopped and turned, and Rebecca said, "Please don't look in the..."

"...toilet cistern, I know."

"In the cabinet," Rebecca said. "You are weird."

The bathroom cabinet was actually very tempting to look in but I really didn't need to know. When I came out, Rebecca had a laptop open and had lit a cigarette.

"I'll see you tonight," she called over. "It's great to see you. Just a surprise. With the clothes and... We can catch up later. I'll book the table in... our name."

"Good one," is all I said, before heaving open the door. No hugs but she hadn't been unfriendly.

Outside on the street, standing under the same sky and breathing the same air as I had for the last forty-nine years, I saw it all –

the plethora of life itself. It looked, sounded, smelled and, as I drew in breath, tasted completely different from anything I had known. It was all hyperreal. A super accurate version of the world I knew, but better. Enhanced. Marylebone High Street was the most ultra-vivid scene. I had never felt this way before. This must be how the lucky ones who know who they are experience things. No wonder they can spot adverts in newspapers. I felt like I could see through walls into buildings and read the thoughts of people passing by. This, I realised, is what exhilaration feels like. And how!

OK, now Harrods. The first thing to say about Harrods is that I didn't go to Harrods. I know, I know, I'm suddenly like this crazy, risk-taking, rule-breaking desperado but I just couldn't do it. I was in a taxi and we were headed to Knightsbridge but it wasn't me. It felt all wrong. It's not every day you are given twenty thousand pounds credit to spend on clothes. And, should it ever happen to you, you would at least want to make the most of it, get some value, for yourself, right? Now I imagine you are thinking: "Oh God, no, she spent it all at Primark." That would have been funny, if it were even possible. That would be like three thousand blouses! Can you imagine how many brown paper shopping bags you would have? Never mind a car, no one gets a car home from Primark! You'd need your own bus (both decks, up and down) just to fit it all in. It would also have been amazing if I had jumped the train home and spent the lot of it in my old store. But of course it is shut now, so that could never happen – the local sixth-form art department are using it as a gallery space. No, I went to Dover Street Market.

One thing I will say, as a disclaimer, about Dover Street Market, is that I know David Sedaris shops there and I know how funny his stories are about buying culottes and tiny bird skeletons. I am definitely not even going to try and compete with him for laughs. I also know, because I read his book too, that John Waters shops there. I urge you to read David Sedaris and John Waters, and me too, if I am so lucky as to be published. I redirected the cab to Dover Street Market because, when Pipa and I had lunch at the Rose Bakery, we had walked down through all the floors, and down again to the basement where I'd bought her a Palace Skateboards shirt, and back up to the ground floor with all the jewellery and sunglasses and the polka dot wallets and, well, that was where I wanted to go. I thought I pretty much had the measure of the place. Harrods, honestly; they'd eat me alive.

Did I for once think that maybe I had a better use for twenty thousand pounds than spending it all on clothes? No. Thirty years in very localised Ladies' Fashions is more than enough of a kick-starter for a day spent swimming in the luxury end of the pool. Did I for once think that this money was very likely illegally gained? Yes, I did. But... I had just found Rebecca again and we had a dinner date and I really, really didn't want to lose her again. Besides, as you will find out, I LOVE CLOTHES!

Now then, Dover Street Market. The shopping itself wasn't hard but it was a lot of work. I arrived at noon and I left at six. I took a break for a superfood salad at Rose Bakery, during which time assistants came up with more and more clothes for me to consider. I had my own VIP personal shopper, who reminded me of Arthur, the cartoon character aardvark, so much so that I now can't remember his real name. By about three in the afternoon, I started buying men's clothes – for myself! There were designers I loved; Sacai, Undercover and Comme des Garçons, but their men's collections were always more 'me' than the women's. Then there were the designers, like Raf Simons, who only did men's; I bought his stuff too. In some of the spaces – and Balenciaga was like this – all the clothes were mixed up on the rails so you didn't know where you were, genderwise. The only way I knew I was buying men's was when I took a garment from the hanger and the assistant would say: "That is actually men's." It did rather defeat the point of their unisex policy but he soon stopped saying it when I kept adding them to the pile anyway. They had Gucci too, but those clothes are so heavily patterned and adorned with logos that it's less like you owning the clothes and more like they own you. All in all, I bought sixty-two items! I can't list everything here, it would just take too long. I thought about simply reprinting the receipt in the book but I measured it against my copy of *Generation X* and it would actually run over ten pages! I held it up and it was as tall as me. Now if someone asks how much I spent, I shall coyly reply, "About five foot seven inches."

There were some real highlights, which I will describe now, because I wore them to dinner at AMA. We can start with the Raf Simons sweater with more holes in it than wool. "Like Polo mints," I said to my personal shopper friend. "What would they be, without the mint they are without?" I wore the sweater over a Comme des Garçons BOYS shirt that fitted like a fitted blouse. I didn't buy a watch because the watch I wanted was Harry Fane Cartier and £12,000, and, you know, when would I have the time to look at the time anyway! I did buy a bracelet by Suzanne Kalen for, ahem, £4,000. Ouch. I bought a lot of shoes and trainers but the ones I chose for AMA were Comme des Garçons black leather lace-ups with a round toe that lifted up a bit from the ground. The shoes and the Bottega Veneta bag were women's, as was the coat from The Row – cashmere and felt like a million dollars, which was a good return on my money, as it only cost £3,700. The trousers, from Undercover, were grey wool flares that had a drawstring waistband like sweatpants. They were definitely men's, as they had a zipper fly. Anyway, you couldn't see the waistband for the jumper and the untucked shirt hanging out. An avant-garde Annie Hall was the best description I could come up with when faced with myself in the mirror at ten to seven that evening. No manicure or facial or any change from £20,000, but I was ready for dinner with Rebecca. I was just going to be a little bit late, that's all. At least this time I wouldn't spend five minutes outside the restaurant trying to find the door.

It is actually now two days after the night spent at AMA. It has taken me that long to write it up. I don't know if you have seen *Dinner With Andre*? It's a film of a dinner. Two people meet for a meal in a restaurant and that's it, the whole film. It's much admired. Roger Ebert has it in his Great Movies list. I like the film myself but, with the greatest respect, it's not exactly *Strictly Ballroom*. My dinner with Rebecca could be a book in itself. It could easily run longer than everything I have written so far. Our meal was twice as long, and a bit more, than *Dinner With Andre*; four and a half hours we talked, non-stop. If I had recorded it, the transcript alone would be a hundred pages. And that would just be the words that were said. Fine for a film script but, here in this book, I'd have to take on the role of the director, lighting, cameraman, make-up, wardrobe, set designer and both actresses – all of that just to get it onto the page. Which is not to say I am not up to the task; I'm loving writing now and I have all day and every day to do it. I just want to keep it in check, that's all. It'll be so much better for a tighter edit.

Anyway, try this on for size:

I arrived fifteen minutes late. I'd walked from Soho to Mayfair, which really is quicker than a cab. The new Comme shoes could have done with a more gradual breaking-in than a power walk across Regent and Bond Street though. There were bloodstains on my socks when I finally got back to Wardour Street at 2am. But at 7.15pm precisely, I entered AMA to the "Irasshaimase" chorus. The restaurant was full already. I scanned the room and there was Rebecca, sat at a table for two in a corner at the back. The chair opposite her was the only unoccupied seat in the room. I mouthed a "Sorry, I'm late." She was watching intently as I handed my coat to the maître d'. I felt her eyes widen and refocus as the grey cashmere gave way to the comically large holes of the

Raf Simons sweater and pink pinstripe of the shirt underneath. My hair was fixed up with a big clip at the back. Hers was down, falling around the shoulders of a black satin tuxedo-style jacket. She had two very low scoop-neck tops, layered, one on top of the other, a wide-mesh camisole over a black satin one of the same cut. I guessed that she would forego the satin underlining for male company. I could see her legs under the table as I approached. She was wearing trousers to match the jacket and wonderful tall, strappy heels. A clutch bag, black with a gold buckle, sat beside her on the banquette. We had been twinned in the morning, now we couldn't have been more mismatched. I located the black American Express card in my purse and, as soon as I was seated, I placed it on her side of the table. "Thank you," I said.

"Dover Street Market," Rebecca said, with a raise of her eyebrows. "I got a text from AmEx."

"Yes. Sorry. I'm not very Harrods."

"I can see that." Rebecca gave the outfit another considered look and a smile lifted her face. "You look amazing. You look…" She seemed lost for words to describe me. "You look really cool," she laughed. "Which is a bit annoying. But good for you. Are you crying?"

I was. I didn't expect that to happen but sometimes what can you do? I was crying and laughing and smiling helplessly as the tears ran down my cheeks. I was crying now without any help from Kate Bush or Nick Cave or Richard Adams (author of *Watership Down*, in case you were wondering). Crying my own tears. Oh God, this was so not the plan. Rebecca waved a waiter away and passed me my own napkin. I pressed the linen to my eyes and held it there, like I was stemming a nosebleed. I felt Rebecca's hands on my arms, around my elbows, her fingers through the holes in my sweater, holding the shirt underneath. She was leaning across the table. I moved the napkin from my eyes and focused on her face, so close to mine.

"I love you," Rebecca said.

It wasn't meant romantically. It was meant to cut across the thirty years of two entirely separate and distinctly different lives, to return us to where we had left off so many years ago. And it worked. I nodded. "Yes," I said, through the tears. "I missed you."

"I missed you too. Like you couldn't know."

I was always riled by the tweenagers on Instagram calling each other best friends forever, friends for life, BFFs, as they say. Well, they have no right to say that aged fourteen. Becky and I, in this moment, could say it, and then it would really mean something.

"Now we are back," Becky said, still holding my arms. "Cagney and Lacey."

"Oh, fuck off," I said, crying and laughing at the same time again. "There's no way I'm..."

"Thelma and Louise, then," Becky corrected herself.

"Better," I said. "Susan Sarandon. Best breasts in Hollywood."

"It's true," Becky agreed. "The woman in *Short Cuts*, though."

"You mean *The Player*. Greta Saatchi. Tim Robbins was in it. He was going out with Susan Sarandon."

"You know your stuff."

"Thirty years, Blockbuster Video and then Amazon Prime."

"Let's order something," Rebecca said, bringing us back to AMA again.

I recovered enough to order pretty much everything I had eaten before with Pipa. There really wasn't anything I didn't like. And I said yes to wine, which Becky chose.

"So who goes first?" Becky asked.

"You do. Let me just listen." And that's what I did. I nodded and said 'and...' and 'wow,' and I laughed and I probably gasped and winced too as she told me her story.

"OK. So I had the gun," Rebecca began. "The one you wouldn't touch. Didn't touch. That's been a test for me that I've used since that night in my bedroom. 'The June test,' I call it. I show someone a gun and if they are scared and won't touch it, well that's them out. If they grab it and point it at me or at anyone, they are out too; a definite no. But if they pick it up and weigh it in their hand, look at it closely and then put it down, then they are in."

"That's why I was out?" I asked.

"Oh you were a definite no. Anyway, that summer I had met Darren. He was the boyfriend you didn't meet. He was twenty-eight. I was nineteen. I got my diploma and we moved to Bracknell – don't ask me why, but he knew someone there – and we slept in the van until I found a job in the head office of a management consultancy company. We got a small flat. He didn't work but he made himself available for... criminal activity. It's not a job you can apply for, as such. He would just spend his days in pubs, chatting to people here and there and eventually he would meet someone who needed something stolen or a building burned down; mostly their own stuff and their own buildings, so they could claim on the insurance. Nothing too serious. My part in this Bonnie and Clyde operation was to do my job and look for opportunities on the inside. These days it would be easy. You'd just hack the computers and move all the money. But this was pre-digital. 1991. The accountants handled the payroll, which was all BACS payments, and I couldn't get close to it. Only the cleaners and security staff were paid in cash. But the company handled this for other companies too and, on one set day in the month, there was fifteen grand in the safe. Pathetic really. That's what we took. £15,000 in cash and for that we left town and went on the run."

"That's when you took my name?"

"No. That was later. We did all this three more times. Swansea, Peterborough, Lincoln – some tour that was. He was drinking heavily, spending much more time in the pub than he was out burning things down or beating people up. Then he beat me up and that's when I shot him. Not dead. I shot a hole in his hand when he tried to grab the gun. But guns and gunshots are serious, you know. He very stupidly went to hospital, a proper NHS one. That got the police involved. He told them it was me. Like, thanks for that – tedious shit. The result of all this being that it was me that disappeared and him that went to prison for various offences. That was 1997. He only had a few years to do and I am sure he would have got out and come looking for me.

But he killed someone else while in prison, for money, no doubt, and got caught for that. So he's not coming out any time soon. And now he knows that even if he did, he'd be dead anyway."

"Dead because…"

"Because… enough people owe me a favour."

"Right," I said.

Becky stopped for a second to eat a few pieces of sashimi from the plate between us. "It only gets worse," she said. "Do you want me to continue?"

"I want to know about my name."

"Right. OK. So I officially disappeared in 1997. I slept rough for a while. Hitchhiked around. I even came home for a few days." She stopped there, realising that that was a mistake.

"Not to see me?"

"I saw my mum. Just so she knew that whatever she'd heard, I was alive."

"So she did know where you were?"

"No. She just knew I wasn't dead. That's all I could do for her then – just not be dead. More recently I've been… well, have you seen the house they live in now?"

I shook my head. I hadn't seen it.

"The one at the end of the road we lived on. The big one. That's where they live now. Least I could do, really."

"But you didn't want to see me when you came home that time?"

"I did. And I did see you," Becky said. "I saw you. You were in the park. It was a summer day. You were with your husband,

I assumed. You had a picnic and a blanket. You were lying with your head in his lap..."

I knew what she was going to say.

"...and you were pregnant."

I closed my eyes. I closed my eyes at the table and I remembered that day and the picnic. I have always been able to remember it a little too well because, in the middle of that afternoon, a boy fell from the climbing frame, straight on his head, from hanging upside down to hitting the tarmac. An ambulance came and later we heard he had broken his collarbone. I was pregnant for the first time and this accident, and the ensuing incident with the ambulance, happened around me like I was somehow integral to it. I thought that this boy might die and my unborn child would live. Like there was any form of connection other than the coincidence of being in the same place. Crazy, I know, but that is how I was thinking. Years later, I always hated it when my sons insisted on playing on that climbing frame.

"Sorry. I really am sorry," Becky said. She was close to tears now. "I saw you so happy. And it broke my heart."

I looked at her now. I reached across the table and took her hand in mine, holding it tight.

"I took the train to London," Becky said. "I never came back. And that is when I took your name. I had to have a name..." Becky was crying now. I kept hold of her hand. "You can't not have a name. And I wanted yours. I suppose you think it was because of the birthdates being so similar, but I only realised later how useful that was. The same day I saw you in the park was the same day I first signed my name as you. At a hostel in Waterloo. They asked my name and I said, 'June'. Because, more than anything, I wanted to be you."

Becky was really crying and, even sat as we were, in the back corner of the room, we were still the centre of attention. She blew her nose loudly into her napkin. That attracted the attention of anyone who had not already been staring at us.

"Fuck 'em," Becky said, a bit too loudly. She realised it and followed it up with a "Sorry," directed to the whole room. She held her hand up, by way of further apology. "Just having a bit of a moment." That seemed to settle people. They turned back to their own rather less emotional meals. Rebecca and I both laughed. Then we laughed at each other. And then laughed histrionically at our histrionic laughing; an infectious loop that took a while to escape from.

"You've got to tell me something now," Rebecca said, wiping her eyes and downing a gulp of wine. "I'll tell you the rest of my story after."

So now it was my turn.

"There's two stories. One very long and very boring and I can tell it very quickly and it will still be boring. I got married and had kids, two boys, and then got divorced and married again. And for the whole time – thirty years – I worked in the same store. More or less the same job. Absolutely nothing happened. I fell off a wall in Holland, actually. That happened."

It was a bit shocking, laying it out like that. I know I have been saying this all the way through the book, but to just explain three decades away in less time than it took Rebecca to pick up, chew and swallow a piece of fish, was a bit ridiculous. Maybe this is what happens when someone takes your name and does so much with it. Like when a computer gets hacked and 95% of the processing power is being used to send millions of spam emails. It happened on my husband's laptop after he downloaded a pirate version of a golf game. Is that what happened to me? I was drained by another vessel?

Rebecca wasn't party to these thoughts, though. "Uh-huh," she said, picking up a piece of white fish that might have been mackerel. "And what's the other story?"

"Well, that is the story of this year. I started writing a book in March. It was just supposed to be all the crazy thoughts and ideas I ever had, but I was seduced into an affair with an eighteen-year-old girl, and together we uncovered a bigamist, who I then used to find you. Then my store was closed down and I lost my job. I was on the TV but upstaged by my friend in a 'Frankie Says' T-shirt. I took the redundancy pay and left my home and husband and came to live here. I'm writing the book."

Rebecca gave me a kind of puzzled questioning look, like she thought maybe that was it, that was all I was going to say.

"Anything in there you want to know more about?" I asked.

"I think you could elaborate on all of it. But..." Rebecca paused to sip her wine, "let's start with the eighteen-year-old girl."

So I told Rebecca the Pipa story. Pretty much as I had written it in the book. If there is one thing you get from honing and crafting 45,000 words, it is fluency. And you can quote yourself without fear of plagiarism. She wanted more detail of the sex than I had written – will ever write in the book – so I told her about that. She had never had any experience with a woman, which was a relief for me, as, while not trying to score points, I did want to bring something of my own to the table. She loved it. I got the feeling that if AMA had raw naked Pipa on the menu, Rebecca wouldn't have waited to order, she'd have been chasing her around the kitchen. Maybe I made it sound too sexy. Maybe it was just pretty damn sexy. I missed Pipa again now.

"Alright," said Rebecca, picking up her clutch, "I need to pee and have a quick fag. Don't go anywhere. Bigamy when I get back."

I fumbled in my bag for my notepad and pen. There were things that came about in the retelling, in my performance and in Rebecca's response, that needed recording. I thought that from now on I would read the book back to myself out loud. This was not something I had been doing before, but I'd ad-libbed some lines that made Rebecca laugh, while other bits didn't work as well as I'd thought they would.

Rebecca returned. "That's better," she said. "Carry on."

So I told her the Peg and Len story. The greenhouse gasses and the look from Peg when I said he seemed like a new man. The Pipa story had been salacious but the two Lens came out as a comedy. I hit a groove. It was like stand-up, albeit for an audience of one (and a few other close tables who were trying hard not to listen, but who could blame them for being hooked into tales of lesbianism and bigamy). Rebecca loved it. She was loud in her responses. "Oh, he's such a fuckin' fuck," she said of Len, when I explained how he had engineered his meeting with Tina. "And you blackmailed him to find me? Genius." "Peggy! I fucking love that woman," she said, when I got to the 'Frankie Says' T-shirt story, before adding a sympathetic "sorry" for me. "Great for the book, though, right?" she said of that episode. "All of this in the book?" I nodded. "This is going to be a smash, no?" I said I hoped so. "Oh, it will be," Rebecca said.

"The best part will be today," I said, waiting for her to realise what that meant.

"Ah," Rebecca said, as it sunk in. "That's going to take some finessing."

I nodded and pursed my lips. Waiting again for Rebecca to say no.

"The turning up in my clothes was pretty good," she said.

More nodding from me.

"You're going to have to change both our names."

"I'm already doing Len twice over."

"Oh, what were his real names?"

I told her. She was thinking hard.

"So the whole Leg and Pen nickname thing?"

"I made that up."

"Pipa and the IKEA lamp."

"All my own work."

"Damn. You're good."

Then, of course, we spent almost a whole hour inventing a name for us to share. I won't tell you all the combinations and permutations, I'm sure this is destabilising enough, to have read this far into a book and discover the author is not who you thought she was, at least not in name. We were Maureen Stuart for a good ten minutes before we both vetoed the 'Mo' shortening. It was a lot of fun. We had to invent Rebecca Shackleton too. I let Rebecca choose Rebecca; it was to be her actual name, after all. June we were going to share, so it had to be agreed by mutual consent. In the end, Rebecca loved the Helmut Newton's wife red herring, a McGuffin, as Hitchcock called them, plus the fact that the real June Newton used a pseudonym herself, Alice Springs, when she was a photographer in the seventies.

"And you're calling it *Best Seller?*"

"Yep."

"I love it."

And then I needed the loo and Rebecca came too, smoking a cigarette out of the tiny window.

"Do you want me to watch you pee, like your girlfriend?" Rebecca asked.

"No I do not! You have to finish your story. Tell me what happened when you came to London," I called out from the cubicle.

"Yeah, yeah, my turn next. It's just not going to be as funny as your story."

"Different genre," I said. "A thriller, I'm guessing."

"True crime," Rebecca said, as I flushed the loo.

We went back to the dining room. It was late now – half eleven – and most of the tables had been cleared. Rebecca went up to the manager and handed him the black AmEx card to run through the machine. She came back and said we had as long as we wanted. She lit a cigarette at the table.

"So I took your name. Same age, more or less. Born in the same city and, no disrespect, but you were leading a very quiet life. You may have hated it, the anonymity, but it played perfectly for me. Even then I struggled to do anything legal. No National Insurance number. I still don't have access to the NHS now. So I stayed underground and worked for the firm. I had the mole removed." Rebecca touched the skin on her cheekbone where the mole used to be.

"You do look a bit different," I said. "I mean in a good way."

"It had to be done by a private surgeon. The firm put the money up for it. I had to work to pay it back. I was a honeytrap for a good few years and good at it. All the perks of being a call girl, but safer in the knowledge that the night would end better for me than it would for the guy. I gave that up when I turned thirty. I don't think I was any less sexy, just the men they set me up with were getting older and older. It went from cocaine to Viagra. Not much fun."

Rebecca lit another cigarette. I drank my wine. Neither of us had eaten more than a starter. There was untouched food all over the table.

I remembered my mum once chiding me, "June, you haven't touched your food," and I precociously touched the tip of my finger to a sprout.

"Then I had my first big break," Rebecca continued. "The

firm always had to launder money – quite a lot of it. So I asked if I could have a go at that. The idea was to open a business, make it look like any other business, and gradually let the money disappear into it."

"I know how it works," I said. "You know Cheez & Toast on Wardour Street? It's closed now."

Rebecca smiled. "That's just a shit name for a shit business. If they were money laundering it would still be open."

"Oh," I said, a little disappointed.

"I opened places all over London and managed them all. Over a hundred premises, at one point."

"Wow."

"The thing was... you are supposed to lose money, right? You drop a hundred grand of dirty money in and after six months you take eighty or ninety out clean. You don't want to lose more than 20% but that's how it's done."

"Go on," I said.

"Turns out I wasn't very good at losing money."

"Oh."

"Everything I did made a profit. Big profits sometimes, which was a problem in itself."

"Because..."

"Because then you have to hide it, or lose it again somewhere else or, worst case scenario, pay tax."

"Ah. And tax means they know who you are."

"Exactly. So I tried harder and harder to open businesses that would fail, but I just kept hitting winners."

"Like... what are we talking about here?"

"First it was internet cafés. Then it was phone shops, screen repair and network unblocking. You remember?"

"Oh yeah." I remembered them.

"Well, that was massive for a while. Then I switched to tanning salons – huge again; nail bars – even bigger. The most money I made was on waxing. You cannot imagine the profit margin on a Brazilian. Forty quid and ten days later, back they come again. Literally, itching for another one."

"That's funny. I mean very funny," I said. Hoping I would remember it tomorrow.

"Eyebrow threading," Rebecca continued. "We had one of those in Westfield."

This was amazing; dizzying, really.

"I kept diversifying, in the hope that I'd finally luck into a losing streak. I thought no one would ever pay £5 for a cupcake – oh yes, they would. Disgusting sour coffee that took three minutes to press out of a steampunk contraption – the hipsters loved it. The latest one is bubble tea. Have you tried that stuff?"

"No."

"It's fucking horrible. You wouldn't think it was possible. We have queues. They actually queue down the street."

"Coffee-flavoured tea," I said, with a shudder.

"That was me!"

"No way!"

"Even the Chinese were pissed with me at that one. Until it started selling."

"You know what you should have done?" I said. "Bought a department store."

"God, you're right. I could have bought your one."

"The only queue we had was for the ladies' bathrooms. Then they'd walk all the way out of the store without buying anything."

"Would have been heaven," Rebecca agreed. "Anyway, after a while there was so much money around, it was getting dangerous. Too much heat on me. All the talk was about phone apps. There was an app for everything. This is like ten years ago. And not everything was Facebook or Twitter, right? For every one of those, there were hundreds, thousands even, that failed. So we shovelled all the money into these start-ups in Hoxton and Shoreditch. All those fucking stupid open-plan offices with table tennis tables and crazy golf courses in the 'breakout space'."

This wasn't anything I knew anything about. So I just listened as Rebecca detailed a series of very successful failures.

"There was one that, if you held the phone up with the camera on," Rebecca mimed it for me, "It would recognise vegetables!"

I really laughed at that.

"My favourite one was for pizza. You told it how many people you were and if you did or didn't like olives, and it showed you the lines to cut so that it could be shared equally. We ran that into the ground pretty quickly and re-let the offices to a kind of eBay on your phone venture." Rebecca had paused.

"And?" I said.

"And that one started working. So I put some of my own money into it."

"Uh-huh."

"Last year it sold," Rebecca paused again. "For £550 million."

"Oh. Shit. How much did you have?"

"18% was mine."

I could do the math. Even after half a bottle of white wine and two sakes on an almost empty stomach, I could work that one out.

"Well done," I said. "That must make you..."

"Quite rich, yes," said Rebecca.

"It's a lot of bubble tea."

"Ha. I've got that coming in on top."

"Must be close to the Rich List," I said, thinking of the annual Sunday Times special that I read every year with great displeasure.

"Oh I'd be there on the women's league table for sure," Rebecca said. "Luckily there are plenty of people who really do want to be on that list that don't quite have the means."

"Wait. So you..."

"Made a deal. They... this other woman, she doesn't mind paying the taxes – it's worth it to her just to be on the list. Getting her name on there just makes her more money anyway."

"You didn't just give it away, though? £90 million?"

"No. No, I still have control of most of it. More than enough of it."

I marvelled at this. Here was Rebecca taking her name off the Sunday Times Rich List and, now, if I ever made the best seller list in the same newspaper, it would also be under a pseudonym – June Newton.

Rebecca must have been having similar thoughts: "You get used to it. The lack of recognition. You find ways to... I don't know, secretly enjoy things."

"But I don't completely understand why you can't just go legit? You could buy yourself out, couldn't you?"

"I don't officially exist," Rebecca said, with half a sigh. This wasn't a new thought for her, obviously. "That's the first problem. If I did come clean, I'd have to enter witness protection, which, frankly, I feel like I've already been through, you know?"

I could see that. She had started all over again once already, with a new name (my name) and identity.

"Or I serve time. Quite a lot of time. There's plenty I have done, or can be connected to, that I've not told you about. My lawyer thinks ten to fifteen years."

A sixty-five-year-old Rebecca walking out of Wormwood Scrubs wasn't easy to picture.

"I couldn't do it," Rebecca said. "Besides, neither witness protection or prison are any guarantee of..."

"Of?"

"Survival."

I looked at Rebecca. She was serious.

"You don't leave the firm. There's always one more favour. A debt of honour to someone, somewhere. Even when you think you are level, they'll do something for you that you didn't ask for, but they do it anyway, so you're indebted again."

"Your old boyfriend Darren?"

"Exactly that. They'd take him out, if they thought they needed something from me. And they always do need something. Lucio, you know, you met half of him earlier?"

"I remember."

"Well, his father knows where he spends his nights. He probably put him up to it. It's all a constant shifting trade-off. But you can't just step off the carousel. They don't shoot women as a rule. But if I broke the rules, I don't know..."

"You really are in danger?"

"Not that I can't sleep. It's Lucio who keeps me up all night," she said with a smile. "Besides, if there is a bullet out there with my name on it..."

"Um, hello," I said. "If there is a bullet out there with *your* name on it, then *I'm* in trouble."

"Good point," said Rebecca. "Better keep your head down."

I went to the bathroom. When I came back, Rebecca had herself all in order, businesslike.

"How much did you get in the redundancy payout?" She asked, very matter of fact.

"Thirty thousand pounds."

"And you plan to live on that?"

"It's only the rent, really, that I have to cover," I said, a little defensively.

"It won't be enough. How much is it?"

"It's Airbnb. It's £120 a day."

Rebecca calculated. "Six months is what you've got."

"There's half the equity in the house..."

She didn't like the sound of that. "You're the marrying type, not me. You've done it twice. But that seems a little tough on your husband, to force him to sell."

She had a point.

"Come and live with me," Rebecca said.

"Oh. No. Thank you but, no. I don't think I could write there. I like the room on Wardour. It works for me."

"OK. Well, I'll make a deal for you on that place. There aren't many landlords in Soho we can't work with."

I didn't really know what "making a deal" meant. At least not a Rebecca-style deal. It was after midnight now and I was flagging a bit. Too tired to put up much of a fight. Sleep was what I needed.

"Keep the card," said Rebecca, pushing the black AmEx back to my side of the table. The bottom edge of it was coated in white powder. So that was why she was so perky all of sudden.

"Use that for shopping," Rebecca said. "Food and clothes. I won't get a text unless you go over five grand in a day."

I really was going to protest but...

"I want to back your book. Invest in you. Like my shopping app, but this time I don't want anything back. Not money. I just to want to see you get it published."

Right. OK. Good. That's what I thought but lacked the energy to say out loud.

"I don't want you to give up," Rebecca added, earnestly.

"No, I won't. It's not so far off being finished."

"Good. And I want you to feel free to just write every day. I don't want you to go home. Stay here and work, see me and make new friends. That's what I want."

This was the cocaine talking, I thought, but it was good to hear nonetheless.

"If it doesn't work out," Rebecca continued, "which it will. But if doesn't, you can come and work with me. That way you know you have a safety net."

This I did respond to: "That's the worst and most dangerous safety net ever! A life in organised crime to fall back on."

"Well, consider it a threat then. You'd better make sure the book is good. And you won't need it."

We were just about done. There was more talk. I don't remember it now. About films, I think. It was just a blur by then. The manager and the maître d' had stayed on late for us and we thanked them profusely. Rebecca fished the small envelope of coke out of her purse.

"Do you want half a line to see you home?" she asked.

"I don't do..."

"There's a first and a last time for everything," Rebecca said. "You can have both of them at once."

So I agreed and watched as Rebecca rolled the AMA receipt into a straw and did her line. Then she cut a smaller line and handed me the card and the straw.

"You didn't buy the McQueen with the zip all the way up then?" Rebecca had suddenly remembered the leather biker dress at the exchange.

"No."

"I might go back for that tomorrow," she said. "Kind of *Matrix*, don't you think?"

We were handed our coats. Hers, a huge fake fur. She had a car outside. I said I would walk, forgetting that the shoes would soon be dicing up the back of my heels. We had a big furry cashmere hug. We kissed. Not like I kissed Pipa. The passion Rebecca and I shared was for each other. Best friends forever.

And then I walked back to the flat, skipping a bit along the way. I smiled at dishevelled strangers, who, for the most part, looked amazed, which is actually a polite way of saying 'deranged'. It was half one in the morning on a weeknight, after all. I got through the front door and up the stairs, took my bloodstained socks off and lay in the bed, wide awake, until 3am. I'd taken my last line of cocaine. Not so many people kicked drugs quite so easily, I thought. And then had to get up again to write that down in my notepad.

JUNE NEWTON

Tuesday 7th December

I could have just left this entry blank. Or not mentioned the date at all and hoped you wouldn't notice. It is, of course, my birthday. It is the other June Newton's assumed birthday too, but, as she and I both know, Rebecca has been fifty for five months already. She is not getting a card from me. If I missed her real birthday, and the thirty birthdays that preceded it, that is hardly my fault. She'd better message me, though. She owes me that. My husband texted last night: *There's a present for you at home.* That was heartbreaking. Just the word 'home' triggered a proper cry. It's obvious that he sent the text the night before, thinking I might go down on the train. I can't. The truth is that I am terrified of going, lest, for some admittedly irrational reason, I can't get back out of there again. I realised I had never bought a return from anywhere other than 'home' in my whole life. And I always used the second ticket. What if that doesn't work from London? What if there was a mix-up at the station when I tried to come back? The old guy at the ticket booth, who I knew quite well, would recognise me and refute the ticket, refusing to believe that 'home' was anywhere other than where I was born. What if he just took the return part and tore it up, right in front of me? This is not, by the way, a dream or a nightmare I had last night; this is me sitting in the flat on Wardour Street, typing it straight onto the laptop screen. A very real fear.

I should also say now that my husband has done absolutely nothing wrong. My first husband hadn't either. The problem is clearly me. The pair of them did nothing wrong, and what they didn't do right, they could hardly be judged on. Even if they had asked me at the time, "What can I do that would be 'right'?" I wouldn't have been able to give them an answer. I didn't know. They didn't know. I don't really know now. Maybe there is no right way to be married to me. And on that thought, I am going for a walk – sharing my birthday with the people of London.

I really must stop from thinking of things for my next book: *Dead Head In A Bag For Life.* It will be set in London, for sure. I know that much. I have been walking early in the mornings and late in the evenings. I have seen Smithfield Meat Market at 7am. That will certainly be the location of someone being stabbed or having their throat slit, their vital fluids merging with the animal blood that runs along the side of the street or sits in puddles on the pavement. The detective on the case (female, same age as me) will have terrible trouble working that one out – on the trail of someone that has murdered a twenty-nine-year-old sow with ginger hair. At night, I like the City of London. The bars shut early at around 10pm and then the streets are empty and you can spy the corporate art in the lobbies and boardrooms of the big banks. An art theft will be involved, for sure, maybe under the decoy cover of an actual bank robbery?

I could also write a guidebook to London's stinkiest alleyways. I love them. There is an especially urinal one (yes, I am using that as an adjective) off St Martin's Lane, which gets narrower as you pass through it – foreboding or forbidding (it's one of the two words, I am sure). The cut-through between Wardour Street and Berwick Street Market is next level, though; it has so much human waste in it that dogs won't even use it. There is so much to write!

Has anyone ever done that? Started to write a follow-up book in the middle of the first? I imagine it must be quite annoying for the reader – so apologies for that. I will stop!

Birthday text from Rebecca:

Sucks, right?

Wednesday 8th December

I spent some time with David today. David is the man I met at Bruno's when I was with Pipa and he was going into the building next door and stopped to tell me the 'no pickle at Cheez & Pickle' story. He and I have been saying hello to each other for a few weeks now. Tonight we shared a table in Bruno's. This happened, just to be completely transparent, because I can see into the café from my flat opposite and spotted him sitting alone. I scurried down the stairs and contrived to bump into him. That is also when I saw that he has a wedding ring, so you can stop with any speculation or optimistic, romantic 'wouldn't that be perfect for this book' kind of thoughts. I certainly did.

David asked what I did and I said that right now I was writing and had almost finished a book. Then he said he was a publisher, but of photographic books, so he couldn't help me directly. But he knew an agent and also someone who was high up at a publishing company (I won't say which one because, if the book is ever published, it will no doubt be with a rival of theirs and that might be awkward). I replied that I was very glad, in that case, that I had told him. He said the first rule of trying to make anything happen was to tell everyone. That's why normal people find creative people so annoying: they won't stop talking about themselves and how brilliant they are. But that is, he said, just what you have to do. When you are a success you can, if you haven't been completely consumed by your own ego, finally shut the fuck up.

He also offered to read the book as it was written thus far. He said, quite understandably I think, that he couldn't recommend me, or my book, to anyone, unless he knew it was good. That was his second rule: don't send people shit recommendations or make lousy introductions. It doesn't come back to haunt you; it just doesn't come back. Do that once and the relationship is over. This all sounded like real proper insider talk and good advice. I was excited. Very excited, actually, but I tried to hide that by taking an interest in his company. He didn't need to be asked about it – a sign of success, I guess. He asked if my book was going to be funny and have big coincidences in it. "Well, yes, I hope it's funny and, yes, don't worry, MASSIVE coincidences," was my reply. That seems to be what he likes. *Tales of the City-*

style, you know. Of course I am now correcting and rewriting the whole book in an absolute frenzy. So apologies if you might have enjoyed anything I have just completely changed, but you can't help me right now, and maybe this man can.

Thursday 16th December

Walking back to Soho from the City this morning, I passed people who I am now imagining as readers of this book. That's a positive thing to do, right? It helps me get a picture of the reader in my mind. It's what a professional writer should be doing, I am telling myself, and not just a ridiculously hopeless expression of my own vanity (which is, of course, what I really think it is). The young woman who held her phone and a half-litre Frappuccino to the side of her head, talking to someone and carrying shopping in the other hand – she could definitely be my reader. The young mum with a double buggy (a split level, baby-over-the-top-of-the-toddler buggy, the like of which we never had in my day) – she could read this book. I saw a few men, of course, who I couldn't possibly imagine reading this, both executive and labourer types. I don't need them anyway. I saw a woman with straight mid-length blonde hair and a cat-like face – tough call but I could win her over. I saw so many young women with takeaway coffees. Honestly, if only women holding Pret or Starbucks coffees in any one moment were my readers, the book would be an enormous global success.

This led me to an unusual thought. I'd like this book to be something someone reads for themselves, of course, but I would really like it to be a book someone reads for someone else. Not a book you read to someone, a book you read *for* someone. You see someone on the street, like any of the women I saw today, and read it for them. And if that is not an original idea, I give up!

Just as I arrived back at Wardour Street, I saw my ultimate perfect reader, right outside my door. She was about thirty, I would guess. She had a pink plastic bag from Superdrug in one hand and was pushing a buggy (just the one child, this time) with the other. Her black puffer jacket was open and underneath, for all the world to see... a WORLD'S BEST DAD T-shirt. I love her! She's my reader. I will dedicate this book to her.

Friday 17th December

Only weekly updates now. I am almost finished writing. David from over the road has read the first draft. He made a lot of corrections. He filled in some gaps in my knowledge. You know where I now say 'Elon Musk' by name? Well, that was originally, 'the electric car guy'. Not important things. It just smoothes out the reading of it. His favourite joke is the mannequins' hands being stolen and leaving no fingerprints. He thinks there should be more conversations with film stars like Winona and Nicolas Cage. I'll have a think about that. I can't make them happen, I told him. They just come, like apparitions. He said in that case

Carrie Fisher would be perfect. That is a good call. He also had a big note about the jump from September to November. He thinks I left too many loose ends and unanswered questions about the last days of the store, about Peg and Len and Pipa, and leaving my house for the last time and the flight (not an actual flight – a train) to London. He says it could do with some clever link-up play involving a touch or two from everyone on the team. I think he just likes this football analogy too much. "Sometimes you have to go route one," I said. "Pogba on the edge of his own area hits a long ball over the top for Rashford to bring down and score." I could teamtalk football too. Anyway, I didn't want to write any more filler and it felt good defending my decisions.

I asked him who he liked best in the book. He said me, which was sweet. And after me, Peggy, which was annoying, but only to be expected. I think I wrote that T-shirt episode a little too well and far too favourably towards Peg. Most importantly, he is going to introduce me to his agent friend by email. And hopefully that will be the start of something. I really do hope so.

Monday 20th December

The birthday present from my husband arrived this morning. This is after I texted my new address to him and my sons. I guess he had realised I wasn't coming back to claim it. The package will have crossed in the post with Christmas presents I sent for the three of them; three pairs of Vilebrequin swimming shorts that can only rival each other in vile patterns and design.

His present to me was quite unexpectedly wonderful – magical, really. A Sony digital voice note recorder. If you search 'gifts for writers' on Google, you'll see it. I suggested that search to my youngest son, after he very kindly asked what I wanted. I'm sure he will have passed the information on to his stepdad. My husband is a very pragmatic person, quite literal when it comes to birthday and Christmas presents. Thankfully not so matter-of-fact as to gift me a set of highlighter pens and a multi-pack of Post-It notes, which are also suggested by that search. That would have been an underwhelming fiftieth birthday present, even for the wife that walked out on him. The voice note recorder I can use on my morning and nightly walks. I'm excited about it. The card that came with it, as well as saying Happy Birthday, said that there was a message on the dictaphone, already recorded. There was. And here it is. Painful to share. But that's what writers do, isn't it? Something that I am now sure my husband will appreciate.

"Hello, love. I miss you. I know it must have been hard with the store closing. That was why I thought you'd left. But I was wrong about that, wasn't I? The store had nothing to do with it. That was the opportunity you needed. One door closes and all that. I have no idea what your life is like now. More fun than here, I'm sure. I miss you so much. I miss the comments you'd make. The way you thought about things and the things you said. The way you said, 'Spoiler Alert,' when putting the icing on a cake. Or when you called Peggy and told her we couldn't come round for dinner because I already had food poisoning. That was funny. You didn't think anyone appreciated you, but I would often find myself in the middle of the afternoon still trying to work out what you'd meant by 'corridor of uncertainty'. When you were out, I would play the CDs you were playing the night before, when I would come in and find you crying. I'd listen to *Pale Blue Eyes* and *This Woman's Work* and Joni Mitchell's *River* just to understand. And I'd cry too. That Joni Mitchell song. Jesus. Saddest Christmas song ever, right? I don't want this Christmas to be sad like that. Have a think about it. I can come up and see you. There must be somewhere I can park. Oh. Fuck. Sorry, scrub that. It doesn't matter about the parking. I'm such an idiot. I'll come and see you. Just let me know. I love you."

Damn. Just the idea of my husband in tears, listening to Joni Mitchell, made me cry a river. I think I may have to stay married. Just for a little while longer.

I called him. He's coming for Christmas on Wardour Street. I'm seeing Rebecca on Christmas Eve, then he is arriving Christmas morning.

"June."

I looked up. "Carrie Fisher? You're a hologram?"

"I am, yes," said Carrie, from the end of my bed. "It was in my deal with Disney. My agent gave them the rights to use me in that last *Star Wars* film in return for my extended use of the technology. It goes beyond life of copyright, obviously. If you have a minute, I've made this appearance to talk about your book."

"You know I am writing a book?"

"Of course," Carrie said. "That's what we do up here. Read unpublished manuscripts and first drafts."

"That's funny."

"It's not a joke. It's work. And most of what we have to read is – what do you call it? Tripe."

"Oh no," I said. "I'm not tripe, am I? Actually, don't answer that. I love *Postcards From The Edge* so much, I don't want to know."

"That's sweet of you," Carrie said. "You don't suck. There, I've said it. I can't help it. We have to read galley proofs and we can't lie. That's life."

"Afterlife," I corrected her, involuntarily.

"You say that, but there's no life after this one. So the word kind of loses its appeal. Some of these books are very long. And forever can seem like an age when you are handed 600 pages on reality television in the 2000s on a Monday morning."

"Bad one. Sorry."

"Yeah, well. Occasionally I get to read something good. Yours was good from the title. Quite jealous of that, actually."

"I'm still amazed no one else has used it," I said.

"Right! Same here," said Carrie. "But I checked for you. And no one else is going to use it either."

That was a relief. As the book had come closer to completion, it had started to worry me.

"I did have an idea for you, though," Carrie said.

"You did? Wow."

"So you want to hear it? We have to ask first. That's the rule."

"I really do. Of course I do."

"OK. So I could foresee some problems – legal problems. When I say foresee, I mean, they really are coming."

"Oh." Now I was worried.

"What you have written incriminates certain people; confirms their criminality. No one is suggesting they aren't criminals. It's just that it'll do them more harm than perhaps you realise."

"Oh, I thought that by changing all the names..."

"That's not going to wash with the police. I'm not talking about Len, by the way, he's going to get found out, one way or another. It's Rebecca. She needs more protection than you've afforded her. The police and judges will be harsh enough but then the people in the circles she moves in, they administer their own justice."

"I can't have that. I can't have her hurt."

"Or killed," Carrie said, solemnly.

"No! No, not that," I said. This wasn't good news. "So I can't publish it at all?"

"Well, you can either wait for Rebecca to pass away naturally. That's maybe thirty or forty years from now and rather relies on you outliving her. And you know that I know, from personal experience, that that is not a very safe bet."

"No. Or... the other option?"

"You can make David the author. I already gave him the idea

of introducing me to you. You are writing the book under an assumed name anyway. Make David the author and have him publish it as a novel."

This was confusing. "So the whole book is fiction? Not just these conversations with film stars, TV characters and holograms?"

"Oh, this conversation is real enough," Carrie said. "But the rest of the book has to be fiction, yes."

I gave this some thought. Carrie fizzled a bit, but I didn't lose her.

"Do you trust me?" Carrie asked.

"Totally."

"Trust me then. Those women you saw on the street. World's Best Dad and the woman with the crazy double buggy..."

"Yes."

"They will believe that it's real," Carrie said. "And every single woman on the street in London holding a takeaway coffee right now, at this very moment, of 8.55am..."

"That's primetime for coffee holding."

"It is! Exactly 275,597 women in fact. They will all know, deep down, that it is all true."

"Wow."

"My pleasure," said Carrie, as she faded. "Got to go."

And with that, she was gone.

Friday 24th December
(Christmas Eve)

A text from Rebecca this morning. I saw it come in on the phone on the preview banner and turned away. I didn't need that. I had seen her only twice since AMA, and both times only briefly. Christmas Eve was to be our big catch-up. Cancelling now wasn't good. It just showed who needed who more. Not that I didn't have other friends in London. There's David, obviously, who may now end up authoring this book. The man in the dry cleaners on Brewer Street is a charmer. I have been seeing a lot of him. It turns out that of the sixty-odd articles of clothing I bought at Dover Street Market, at least fifty of them are dry clean only, and the ones that aren't are bags and shoes. I just give everything to him, my underwear included. It's worth it for the conversation. I also chat regularly to Claudio, the waiter at Bruno's. It's not the most meaningful dialogue, as he does just agree with everything I say, but it is cheerful enough. Howard Jacobson and his wife I saw again yesterday. Now we do say hello but I have yet to pluck up the courage to take it any further. Imagine if he read my writing. He won the Booker Prize.

Another text from Rebecca and this time I read it. It is not actually from Rebecca. It is, as the first one turned out to be as well, from Lucio. Rebecca is ill. She has been in bed with severe stomach pain for four days. I called him back. I'm still old-school that way. He will be twenty-something, I imagine, and has probably only ever taken twenty-something actual phone calls his whole life.

"She is very sick," he said.

"Can you pass the phone to Rebecca?"

There was a delay. I could hear her "Aaargh" as, very likely, she tried to sit herself up.

"Rebecca."

"Ugh."

"What is it?"

"Poison. Stomach. Aaargh."

She was gone. Lucio came back on the line: "I think it is food poisoning." Then there was another gap. He was walking out of earshot. "She thinks she has been poisoned. You know, by someone."

"Has she seen a doctor?"

"She won't. She says the doctor is one of them."

"What?"

"From the firm. They have their own doctors."

"She doesn't have a normal doctor?"

"She says, no, she is not NHS."

"Bloody hell. I'll come round."

I arrived by cab in half an hour. Rebecca looked bad; very thin, very frail, much older, and her skin was grey like grits (I'd only witnessed grits once and not forgotten it). They had made one of the sofas up as a bed. Rebecca was in a lot of pain. Clearly in agony. She was going to have to go to hospital.

"She has not eaten for four days," Lucio said. "I wasn't here the whole time. I just arrived last night. She had left the door open."

I sat on the bed beside Rebecca. "Can you walk?"

"I have been carrying her to the bathroom," Lucio said. "But no pee," he added.

"Not the hospital," Rebecca moaned.

Lucio explained that the hospital where she had her insurance was a private one very close by, but she wouldn't go as it was the firm, again, that paid for it.

"We have to take her to A&E. It doesn't matter who you are. They don't turn people away."

"But NHS," Rebecca managed to say. "No medical card."

"You don't show a membership card to go to hospital. It's not the Groucho Club."

"But they'll find out who I am. My blood."

"You can be me, OK? Married. Two children."

I took my wedding band off my finger and placed it on hers. It just about fit. She smiled at it there on her hand.

"There," I said. "You wanted to be me. Now you can be."

I put my arms around and under her, to see if I could lift her.

"Icicle Works," said Rebecca.

"What?"

"I just died in your arms tonight."

She's delirious, I thought. "It's not Icicle Works. It was…"

Rebecca cried in pain as I moved her. "Cutting Crew," I said, remembering the band. "And, anyway, it's a love song."

"That's good," sighed Rebecca. "That's alright then."

I held her for a minute. Just as I had imagined her holding me back in the summer. Now I could comfort her. But not for as long as I wanted, we had to get her to hospital.

The nearest A&E was UCH at Euston. Less than a mile. We could go in a cab. It wasn't me carrying her, though, even without food for four days, she was still too heavy for me. So Lucio lifted her up. She could just not die in his arms tonight. I looked around the apartment for anything she might want us to take but decided against it. The last thing we needed was to inadvertently smuggle drugs or a concealed weapon into the hospital. She had my wedding band. Jesus, if she needed a kidney, I thought, I'd give it to her. She can have my purse and phone. That would help with the identity crisis.

On the street, a cab driver swerved to pick us up. You get that kind of service with a half-dead woman in a man's arms. A&E was fast. A wheelchair was provided and Rebecca was pushed straight through to triage. One of us could go with her. That would be me. I told them we were sisters. Lucio gave me his number and slunk into a chair in the waiting room. Rebecca was placed on a stretcher bed and the screen was drawn around her. I stayed inside the curtain and held her hand. Tests were done and blood was taken. I texted Lucio to tell him she was having tests. He texted back: *Poison?* I didn't reply. I didn't know.

We had been in the hospital an hour when Rebecca was transferred to a ward. Her bag (my bag) was handed back to me for safekeeping. The porters bumped the bed through multiple sets of double doors as I followed behind. Corridors of uncertainty, I said to myself. I couldn't go with her in the porters' lift, as they were staff only. Instead I took the stairs, passing a pair of doctors deep in consultation over a clipboard. That can't be good news for someone, I thought, when your doctors have to consult in a stairwell.

Rebecca must have been screened off somewhere on this third floor ward. I couldn't find her where she was supposed to be and checked the bay next to her. I wished I hadn't. It was a woman with half a leg. No disrespect to her but that was an absolute horror show! I hope she made a full recovery – she couldn't make a full leg recovery, obviously; that would be impossible, but whatever the best that could be hoped for was. I didn't peek round any more curtains. I went back to the sister and asked her where Rebecca was. She had her on her list but looked confused and then she, in turn, asked another nurse.

"In theatre," that nurse said.

"Gone up already," my nurse said to me.

"Where?"

"Fourth floor. You can't go in. They have waiting rooms for family, though."

So that's where I sat. No television. Nothing other than NHS pamphlets, which I couldn't bring myself to read but I did look at the pictures, which was surely worse. I regretted that thought I'd had about surviving cancer now. That was inappropriate. But it can stay in now that I've apologised for it. I hadn't brought a phone charger either and I had no idea how long I'd be here. I didn't know what was happening to Rebecca or what she had been diagnosed with. Not a fucking clue. I texted Lucio with an update. Told him go for a walk or go home, if he wanted to. I texted my husband before the battery died. He was due to arrive at ten, tomorrow morning. Christmas Day.

I'm at the hospital. My friend is in theatre. All happened very fast.

He replied straight away.

Sorry to hear. You don't want me to come?

I didn't reply straight away. He should know that I wouldn't lie about something like that. But, still, it looked like a get-out from me. He was probably having his own similar thoughts; that I wouldn't be lying and he'd look bad if he called me out on it. I was about to reply, when a surgeon passed by in full scrubs.

"Hey," I called out. He didn't stop. I jumped up and scrambled down the corridor after him. I caught him just before the doors to the theatre. "June Newton?" I asked, adding, "I'm her sister."

The surgeon held his pass up to unlock the door and then, with his foot wedged in it, turned to me. "She's in pre-op for anaesthesia. We are backed up. Could be a while before she goes into surgery."

"But, sorry, what's wrong with her?"

"No one told you?"

"I took the stairs and she was in surgery. Please."

The plaintive "please" was the tipping point. He looked at his own clipboard.

"She's not my patient but... suspected poisoning. Oh, no, sorry, that's patient self-diagnosis. It's not that at all. Infection to the stomach."

"That's enough to need an operation?"

"Not on its own," he said. "I'll have someone come out and explain. You can wait. There's a family room."

He pointed me back to where I had been.

"I know it," I said.

For an hour, I waited in the family room, which, this time, I was sharing with an actual family. Romanian, I figured them to be. They were taking things – things of their own – from the little fridge and making up plates for their kids. How long must they have been coming here, I wondered, to set up house? I texted my husband with the last bar of the battery.

Sorry. It's hectic. Yes, come. I'll let you know where I'll be.

A consultant appeared at the doorway. "Jane Newton?" he asked. I jumped up. He led me to a room next door and we sat down.

"Your sister has a stomach infection. Probably quite a rare one. It is unusual."

"It's not poisoning?"

"No!" he said. "What is it with that? Not a spy, is she? That's all she could say when she could speak. She's gone under now. We just need to open her up and have a look in there. Drain the fluid."

"That doesn't sound too bad," I said hopefully.

The consultant pulled a face. Are they allowed to do that: to grimace?

"The danger is that her blood is infected. It's called sepsis. Maybe you have read about it?"

I had read about it. There had been a real drive to educate people about it. I try to avoid reading anything medical if I can help it, those awful leaflets included, but a month or two back "Bigger killer than heart disease *and* cancer" was clickbait on the BBC website.

"One in three people in hospital with sepsis will die from it." This was me speaking, not the consultant. That was the other killer fact I remembered. He nodded. Oh, great.

"The statistic is a little better in this hospital than the national average," he said. "We are on high alert for it. It was a good thing you brought her in when you did. That may well have saved her life." He looked at his watch. I could read it upside down. 6.30pm already.

"She won't go in for a few hours yet. Then recovery and ICU. You can visit her in the morning. She probably won't be speaking, even then. Now you should go home."

"I don't know. That family room is so comfortable," I said. Where did I find the inspiration to be sarcastic?

"It's Christmas Eve," the consultant reminded me.

"Right."

"We will call you if anything happens. Anything other than what we hope will happen, I mean."

"OK."

"And her husband and..." he checked his notes, "two sons. They don't live with her in..."

"Soho."

"Soho, yes."

"No."

This is the best I can do – just write out the dialogue. What he said and what I said. It is hard to think of much more. It would be too messy to describe all the conflicting thoughts. The concern for Rebecca was sharp, like a knife stab, but then there was the other pain; the hurt I felt and the hurt I had caused to my husband. And all the play-acting over our identities was so confusing. What a mess it all was. Stepping out of the hospital, walking down Tottenham Court Road to Soho, thoughts of a life without Rebecca flooded over me: the credit card I had; her blacked-out flat in Marylebone; all the money that would be lost to the woman on the Sunday Times Rich List. Selfish and unhelpful thoughts, these were. My phone was out of battery. It would just be me and the evening of Christmas Eve until I could get back to the flat and recharge. Mental strength was what was required. Negativity must be vanquished.

I stopped at Goodge Street and sat on a wall. Tour guides tell you to look up in towns and cities to see the history of the place. You can see the names of the original businesses and buildings above the signage of the coffee chains and charity shops. Well, on June's tours, you can also look down at your feet and see the past in action. Case in point, right here by the churchyard: hundreds of 'balloons', those small silver nitrous oxide capsules, scattered everywhere. It may only be a few hours back in time but by the look of the pavement this was a historic night, for sure.

I was trying to distract myself. But, sadly, my brain is not a fortress and even when I was back on the move, I was walking too slowly to outpace all the negative thoughts. I stopped again outside Tottenham Court Road station and came to some form of resolution. Death should really be a win-win, I decided. If you believe in the afterlife then you have that to enjoy. And if there is nothing, then no regrets and no looking back. If I really think about it, on a personal level, I am less scared of death than I am not keen about not being alive.

Saturday 25th December
(Christmas Day)

I was at the hospital before 9am. I had to wait outside ICU before I could visit. Then it was full-on hand sanitiser and protective clothing; the risk of infection was so high. Rebecca was in a room of her own. A super-wired, dripped, monitored, beeping, bleeping techno chamber (orchestra). She was asleep but she was also alive, which was all that really mattered. They gave me fifteen minutes. There wasn't much point staying longer, they explained. It would be a good few hours before I could expect her to acknowledge my presence, let alone speak. In the meantime, she was not expected to die. Phew.

The hospital café wasn't open; it was Christmas Day, after all. Vending machine Nescafé and a Snickers bar was breakfast. My husband called. He had parked the car in Regent's Park. You had to pay by text message. He couldn't tell if he had to pay today, but he paid anyway. This kind of idle middle-aged, mid-life chit-chat was actually just what I needed. He was so thrilled that the Congestion Charge was suspended for Christmas that, foregoing any concern for Rebecca he may have had, he couldn't help telling me about it anyway.

"Hey," I said, "save some of this gold! I'll see you in ten minutes. If you use up all your traffic talk now, you'll have nothing to say."

We met at Great Portland Street tube. Him, walking to towards me in the North Face jacket, jumper and jeans I was so familiar with. Me, waiting for him in a chaos of clothes from Undercover, Sacai and The Row that, theoretically, he could have been familiar with if he looked at fashion magazines, which, theoretically or otherwise, he didn't.

"You've taken the ring off," was the first thing he said. Super-observant, I thought. But it was probably the first thing he'd planned to check on.

"I've got some explaining to do," I said, taking his left hand in mine, interlocking our fingers so his ring sat next to where mine should have been. "But don't worry. The ring is being taken care of – very intensive care is being taken of it right now."

He looked confused.

"It's going to pull through," I said, continuing my crypticism. Back with the red underline for 'crypticism'! I am going to turn the spell check off! It can't keep up with me.

We walked through the Rose Garden in Regent's Park. It was

Christmas Day in the most beautiful park in London but, alas, it didn't snow. I could have pretended that it did. You can pretend that it did, if you want. I really don't mind. When this book is published, I won't be precious about it. "Who do you want to play you in the movie?" they'll ask. "Marion Cotillard or Carey Mulligan?" "Oh, I'll let you decide," will be my reply. Like it's going to be anyone other than Olivia Colman, anyway. She plays everyone.

I told my husband about Pipa. He had to know before the book came out. He walked along beside me in silence for a while.

"I think I'm alright with that," he said. "If it was another man, it would be different. But it wasn't and you didn't fall in love with her. And she dumped you and…"

"And what?" I asked.

"It's very sexy."

I kissed him. Properly. Where is that snow when you need it?

"That's a very typical male clichéd thing to say," I said, giving it the full false admonishment. He smiled haplessly.

"I won't be moving back home," I underlined, as we continued walking.

"No. But I could come up for the weekend now and again."

"Dirty weekends in London with your wife?"

"Yeah."

"Yeah."

We stopped back in at the hospital. Thankfully, my husband didn't have to play the role of Mr Rebecca. He hadn't fully got his head round the whole assumed names business, or the layers of disguise and subterfuge that applied to her NHS status or otherwise. Rebecca had her eyes open. She couldn't speak. At least, not properly. She managed a few genuinely terrifying attempts. Apparently the surgeons had pressed down on her throat during the operation. I'm not sure why; to stop her from vomiting, I guess. Anyway, it gave a Rebecca a monstrous rasping voice like a cross between Darth Vader and both of Marge's sisters in *The Simpsons*.

"That's not her usual voice," I deadpanned for my husband.

"WHOOO..." That sound, that was also a question, came from Rebecca. It was directed at me in reference to my husband. Of course, they had never met before.

"My husband," I said, as if speaking to someone very young or very, very old. I gave him a kiss on the cheek, in an attempt to illustrate the fact that we were married, you know, like you might have had to do for a very Catholic guesthouse proprietor in Italy in the seventies. Rebecca rolled her eyes at this demonstration of matrimony. That's not just a writerly expression, by the way. Her eyes actually rolled round in her head so that only the whites were showing, and stayed that way.

"It's how she'd like you to remember her," I said to my husband. He looked down at the urine filling up the plastic pouch at the bottom of the bed. "That too," I said. "Very her. Always with the latest bag by her side." There was something about hospitals and illness that made me strangely acerbic. Classic defence mechanism, I am sure.

We left Rebecca and headed out, past the ICU reception. A man was stood up against the desk of the duty nurse. It was clearly 'a scene' – other staff had turned to look at him as he challenged the nurse. "No. I told you. Her name is Rebecca," he said. He had the most horrible tone of voice. I froze. My husband stopped a pace ahead of me. I was looking beyond him at the man at the counter. He only had a T-shirt on and jeans. A thin blue plastic bag swung from his left hand, held only by his first two fingers and thumb. The other two fingers were disjointed and limp. The back of his hand was marked with a deep red scar. Oh, fuck. This was Darren. It must be. And this was danger. The plastic bag was weighted down heavily. That could be a gun.

"You can't see her," the nurse said. "Only family. Her sister is visiting now, if you..."

"She doesn't have a sister," the man said, with a revolting drawl, like Johnny Rotten being interviewed on television. Disdainful and menacing.

I tugged on my husband's jacket sleeve and pulled him round the corner of a wall.

"Shush," I commanded him. "Listen."

"Sir," the nurse said, louder now. "You have to leave. If not I will have to call security."

"I'll find her myself," the man declared.

"Quick. See if he is coming," I whispered to my husband.

He stepped out from the corner and turned back to me. "He's heading up the other way. Looks like the nurse is calling security."

"We have to be quick," I said. "That's Rebecca's ex. He's out of prison. He'll kill her."

"Jesus. OK. Um... I'll guard Rebecca. You see that security get here. Should we call the police?"

"I don't think we can," I said. This had to be dealt with some other way. "You go to Rebecca. I'll call someone."

My husband headed back to Rebecca's room. I stepped into the hall and saw Darren walking away down the corridor, looking in each room as he passed them. I called Lucio.

"June," he answered immediately. "Is she OK?"

"Yes, but you have to help. Her ex, Darren, is here at the hospital. He is out of prison. He is looking for her. I think he has a gun. Can you call your dad?"

"Fuck, yes. Right now. What floor?"

"Fourth floor, ICU. He has a scar on his hand. Where she shot him."

"Yes. I know," Lucio said. "I need ten minutes."

He hung up the call. I looked back up the corridor. Darren had disappeared. In the reception, two security guards had arrived. The nurse sent them down the corridor where Darren was last seen. I went up to the nurse and pointed to where the guards were walking. "Does that corridor lead anywhere?"

"It goes right round," she said.

"Round the whole floor?"

"It loops back to here," she said, gesturing behind her.

Shit.

"Oh God," said the nurse. Not to me, mind – in response to her screen. "Oh no." She picked up the radio. "Security. Emergency, ICU. Emergency."

I stared at her screen flashing red.

"Doctor Khan!" The nurse called out across the floor to a doctor exiting one of the rooms. "There's a guy ripping out monitors. Rooms 44, 45, 48. Quick."

"Fuck," exclaimed the doctor and ran down the corridor.

"He came for your sister," the nurse said to me, as if this was all my fault. And then she too sped off up the corridor. I turned and ran back round to Rebecca's room. There was my husband standing at the door. He gave me a nod. I nodded back and returned to the reception. I could hear desperate instructions being shouted out from the other end of the floor. The nurse's screen was half red and half green now. They must be plugging patients back in as Darren unplugged more. I had no idea what to do. There was no one else there. I went to call Lucio again. Five minutes now since I'd called him. Surely security would have caught up with Darren by now. I couldn't call Lucio back yet, could I? Who else did I know? No one. And then... Darren appeared.

He stood there, behind reception. And he looked right at me. I stared back at him. There was no pretence about the gun now. The blue plastic bag was wrapped around it but it was in his right hand and his finger was on the trigger. He held it down to his side. But it was all I could look at.

"Where's June Newton?" he asked me.

"I don't know," I said.

"Who are you?" he asked.

Behind him, two security guards appeared. Another guard

appeared from the first corridor and then a doctor. Two nurses looked out through the blinds in one of the private rooms. This was like a scene in a western.

"Nobody fucking move," Darren said, holding the plastic-wrapped gun up so everyone could see it. "Where is Rebecca Shackleton?" he demanded.

No one answered him. I thought I could hear sirens. I really wished I could hear them.

"Where is she?" Darren asked again, turning slowly to make eye contact with everyone.

"We don't know who you are talking about," a doctor said. "She's not our patient."

"You know, though," said Darren, directly to me. "Don't you?" He raised the gun and pointed it straight at me as he walked towards me. "You know where she is," he drawled. The gun was in my face now.

"He means June. June Newton." This was the duty nurse, who had reappeared.

"No," I said, loudly to everyone. "He doesn't. He can't do. Because... I am June Newton." I looked over the gun at Darren and addressed him alone. "Rebecca is my friend. And she doesn't want to see you."

Darren stared back at me. "She had a friend called June."

"She still does," I said.

"Where is she?"

"I'm not going to tell you."

I stared straight at him. Then his eyes flashed left and right and back to meet mine. He moved the gun barrel by just a few degrees to the dead centre of my eyes and I absolutely knew that was it. I saw his eyes sharpen and his finger flex. I knew it had happened before it happened and as it happened. I fully experienced it, the moment of my own death, right up to the fraction of a split second before...

He fell. This horrible man fell forwards and onto me, and I fell backwards into the arms of my husband, who in turn fell back onto the floor. I didn't even know he had come up behind me. I looked up and maybe I saw Lucio and maybe I didn't, and maybe I saw someone else and maybe I didn't, but I felt like I saw somebody turn and head out through the fire escape and I felt like it was Lucio. And right in front of me, face down on the floor, was Darren. Dead. Or as good as, with a crossbow dart in the back of his head.

We were together at the Soho flat by the early evening, my husband and I. Just the five hours with the police and I'm not for a minute thinking that will be the end of it. I must have confused them because I confused myself. And I hope my first husband doesn't get hassled too much because, of course, the crossbow method of execution had made me think of him and his battle reenacting weekends. I couldn't stop talking about him. I hope he has a good alibi. I didn't get a call or text from Lucio either. And I didn't send him one. That felt like the professional thing to do. I mean, why else would he not want to know what had happened, other than he already knew what had happened? And

Carrie Fisher was certainly right when she said she foresaw legal problems. I'm pretty sure I left the police thinking there were two June Newtons when of course there are none. What a mess! It's David's debut novel now, for sure. It all got far too 'fictional' back there at the hospital for me. Right now, I don't even know if Darren is dead or alive. It doesn't seem quite real. All excellent practise for the work I will be doing on *Dead Head In A Bag For Life*, I am sure. Must make sure to see that all fictional goings-on have consequences, though. Without them, no one will believe you :)

It still was Christmas Day, of course. Cosied up in Wardour Street, my husband and I opened our presents. He had brought with him the gift that I had posted to him.

"Just what I need," he said of the Vilebrequin swim shorts.

"You can take them back if they're not loud enough," I said. His present to me was The Jesus And Mary Chain's *Psychocandy* album on vinyl; a record I used to own, a long time ago.

"You could try taking that back for not being loud enough. But I don't think they'd believe you," he said. "There's a record player too," he added. "But that's being delivered. I bought it online."

I'd never known him to bestow such great gifts.

"There's a bottle of Eisberg in the fridge," I said.

"Thank you. I did bring some," he said, looking up the street. "But it's in the car."

I lay back on the bed, propped up by two pillows. I liked having him there at the window. He didn't spoil the view one bit.

"So you live here alone?" he said.

"What?" I said.

"No one else lives here?"

I was confused. Suddenly he was questioning me?

"Here," he repeated, gesturing out of the window.

Oh, he meant Soho! The streets were completely empty. The traffic lights on the crossing by Starbucks would still go red every two minutes: they were programmed to stem the constant flow of traffic. There were no cars tonight, though. I hadn't thought about it before; it's usually always incredibly busy but, in truth, not that many people actually live in Soho.

"I think the people who live here have second homes in the country," I said.

He turned and looked at me. "So do you," he said.

I let that rather comforting thought sit there for a while. "Yes," I said. "So I do."

JUNE NEWTON

Monday 27th December

A quiet morning. My husband has gone home. Rebecca is definitely alive (that status now unlikely to change) and I'll visit her soon. Right now I am watching Wardour Street from my window, looking out for a few more of my favourite things. I never know what they are going to be, these favourite things, but they never fail to arrive.

Right on cue, a woman in hijab and black robes walks down Peter Street, carrying, in one hand, a tray of three tall iced coffees. And it's freezing out. Across her path, cycling the wrong way down the road, is a young father. He might be Japanese. He has one of those modern Scandinavian bikes, where it looks like a small boat at the front. Stowed under the canopy are two children. The smallest is asleep on the shoulder of what must be an older sister. This girl, who herself is not so old, maybe six or seven, is reading a book. She'll have been given it for Christmas, I thought. It must be a very good book, for her to need to be reading it on a bicycle ride the wrong way down Wardour Street. The girl is absorbed. I can tell, from how she is holding the book, that she is much more than halfway through. In fact, she has nearly finished it. Almost at the end.

Thank you. My story continues but, for now, you can stop reading and put the book down.

June

JUNE NEWTON

June Newton found an agent and a publisher and was spared a life of crime.

Rebecca Shackleton/June Newton recovered from sepsis and potential assassination and continues to lead a life of crime.

Pipa Martin moved to London and works in a skate shop in Covent Garden.

Len Hutchins was arrested for bigamy and handed a suspended sentence. He lives with his one surviving wife, Peggy, and is writing his memoir: *You Only Live Once Or Twice.*

Tina Brighton can be found on YouTube via her channel: *Apply Yourself/Appliqué Yourself!*

Brian Boyd Williams was promised an entry in these credits and can be booked for Aircuts (£50) at his own salon in Marylebone, *Née Bryony.*

June's husband visits Soho on weekends. They listen to records.

Names have been changed to protect the guilty.

JUNE NEWTON

Appendix

I know sometimes it is a little bit sad when a book you have been reading and enjoying simply stops. It's fine when you have just read, for example, the first *Tales Of The City* book; you can jump straight to the next one in the series. But this book has no sequel and it will take me some time before *Dead Head In A Bag For Life* is even close to a first draft. So here, instead, are some extra bits I wrote for the start of this book and then cut when it turned out that there was a proper story to tell, after all. They are two true stories of two truly shocking holidays. One can be like a hidden bonus track on a CD and the other like the funny extra part you get in the cinema if you sit all the way to the end of the credits. Thank you for not leaving.

This is the account of the first cheaper-than-staying-at-home holiday I took with my first husband. £89 each for flights to Morocco and seven nights in a five-star hotel. How could you not? Well, here's why we shouldn't have. On the first morning we went to the beach and I wore a swimsuit. My husband said I should cover up but I stubbornly refused. I was in my late twenties then and had a beach-ready body. I'd already compromised by not wearing a bikini. That's the way I saw it. All went swimmingly (you could say) for at least five minutes. Then three men who had walked past us once, walked back past again. One of them stopped, turned on his heel, spat out something short and sharp in Arabic and kicked sand in my husband's face. We didn't know what he'd said but we'd have guessed at something along the lines of, "Cover up your whore." Ashamed, I pulled the towel out from under myself and wrapped it round me. The Moroccan men walked away. And then my husband and I started our first argument.

The afternoon was spent in the souk, where we learned how to barter and bought a carpet for twice what we paid for the whole holiday. It was a rug, of course, not a carpet, but still about 7ft square. The seller said he would deliver it to our hotel. I wasn't so sure we could trust him and insisted we carry it. Then our second argument began. We carried it between us. He carried it on his own. I carried it myself (not for very long) and we carried it between us again, over our shoulders in single file. We were lost. It was hot. At one point he suggested we dump it. Later we would wish we had. Eventually we found the hotel.

The next morning was spent at the pool. At the hotel you could wear a swimsuit and there was no sand to kick in our faces. But no one was swimming. We weren't sure why. I thought I could see something glinting at the bottom of the pool. It looked like a watch. My husband got up, put his sunglasses down on the lounger, stepped forward and dived in. Then nothing. And nothing again. And then I was screaming. He didn't come back up. A waiter ran and jumped into the water. A lifesaver ring was thrown from a balcony. My husband was pulled from the pool. The concierge from the reception desk was on his knees giving him mouth-to-mouth, then pumping his chest. His heart had stopped. The waiter reassured me he would be OK. He said the water was just two degrees above freezing and that is why nobody was swimming. And then water came gurgling up from my husband's lungs and he was breathing again. They covered him in towels and robes. The waiter used the long-handled pool-cleaning net to fish out the watch. "It is still ticking," he said, as if that was the miracle. Luckily, my husband was still showing the correct time as well.

You don't want to hear about the next five days and I don't want to tell you. It wasn't a lot of fun. The final morning eventually came and we took a taxi to the airport. We checked in with our two carry-on cases and then came the rug. It was oversize baggage. It had to go in the hold. The excess fee was £85. As my husband said, the trip had already nearly cost him his life so we may as well pay it. We really shouldn't have. We waited and waited beside the carousel at Gatwick for that rug. It never came. Then we were told that surfboards and skis and stupid things like carpets were over on the other side of the reclaim hall. That was when we saw the man heading out of the baggage area, through nothing to declare, with a rug under his arm. It always amazes me that more luggage isn't stolen. It would be so easy to do. Maybe it is, and no thief ever wanted to gamble on my shabby case containing anything valuable. Anyway, we ran after the man, you know, as much as you can run through customs without raising suspicion. Through arrivals we chased him. Then down the escalators to the train platforms, where he stepped onto the train and we jumped through the doors a few carriages down.

The first problem was that this wasn't our train. This was the Gatwick Express into London: totally the wrong direction and also a premium-ticket service. The second more troubling problem was tackling the thief. He was sitting on the rolled up rug in the carriage with the bicycle racks. My husband, who had been humiliated on the beach and brought back from the dead at the pool, wasn't going into this face-off alone. So we both approached him and began with a reasonably reasonable, "I think that's our rug you are sitting on." That was a split second or so before we both realised that it wasn't our rug. It was a completely different colour, much smaller and, well, basically, his rug and not ours.

Holland. The year 2000. £80 each. It was our only holiday that year and it was all we could afford. Our first son was eighteen months old and too young to know what holidays were and also, unless scientists have since proven otherwise, also too young to experience the peer pressure that would pervade the rest of his childhood. He was left with my parents while we took a well-earned break. Although, if we had 'earned it' a little better, we could have afforded a whole week. The five-day away-break for £80 (being £16 a day) was via train to Harwich and then the overnight ferry to the Hook of Holland. This was followed by two cross-country trains to the middle of the Netherlands, also known as the middle of nowhere. The town was called Apeldoorn. No one I have ever met has heard of it. It is synonymous with anonymous.

On our arrival, it did actually appear that humans had discovered the area thousands of years before; they just hadn't bothered to tell anyone else. We had three days to spend in Apeldoorn (the other two were travelling to Apeldoorn and home again) and a whole itinerary of absolutely nothing to do. At the nearby town of Deventer, the world's largest secondhand book market was held on the first Sunday of August. Of course we were in Holland in the last week of July. You don't get the world's largest book fair for £80 a head, that's for sure; you get Apeldoorn. We could tell it wasn't a popular tourist destination because the only postcards in the shops were the blank ones they sell in packs at Rymans. I bought a pack and some coloured pencils and sketched my own views of the town on the front. One of them I kept blank and described it as 'Apeldoorn in the snow.' That one I sent to my old friend Becky, who was one of the few people I ever knew with a sense of humour. There was never any chance that Becky would be living at the address she had given me thirty years ago. I knew that. I just always sent a card. The rest of the postcard pack I kept in case I ever entered any competitions. I still have them now, in a kitchen drawer at home, twenty years later. I have not entered any competitions. Even if I started now, entry would surely be via email or text. It has all passed me by. People will occasionally say that I look younger than my forty-nine years, but the truth is that, should anyone ever saw me in half, 'Answers on a postcard please' would be written around one of the rings in my torso. Along with 'Ooh, I could crush a grape,' and the 'Blankety Blank cheque book and pen.' These television catchphrases age me indelibly.

The boredom of Apeldoorn wasn't the reason why time moved so inexorably slowly, but it probably was the reason that I drank almost a whole bottle of wine at dinner on Friday night, swam in a lake near the hotel and, at the end of the night, shuffled along a ledge to see, as my husband had thought he had seen, a naked man in one of the hotel rooms. The fact is that I only spent around six or seven hours sober and brain-functioning in Apeldoorn. I would never know the sight of that naked man or, indeed, if he were real at all, because, without a hint of a warning, I fell backwards off the ledge and onto the back of my head. For full disclosure, I fell from a very low wall of about two feet. But at five-foot-seven, rocking on my heels and falling straight back, it was certainly enough to knock me out and, as I found out later, shove my brain forwards against my skull. Semi-conscious I was then delivered, in a siren-wailing ambulance, to a hospital about twenty miles further into deepest nowhere. I spent the night in a coma. The doctors instructed my husband to telephone my parents and relay to them, in the middle of the night, that there was at least some chance I would not make it to see the morning.

I woke up in what I now know to have been an intensive care unit. At the time, however, with my eyes seemingly sealed shut and alien objects running up my nose and down my throat (and having no memory of the accident to give me any context), I honestly assumed I was in hell. It was genuinely terrifying, I can tell you. Only someone who has been knocked out, zipped up in a body bag and thrown from a bridge into the freezing cold water of a river, could have had it worse. And if anyone has survived such an experience, I really would urge them to write a book. I would certainly buy it, even it was bad – just out of respect.

Later that day – at least I think it was – I was moved to a room off to the side of a ward. I couldn't walk. I couldn't really sit up or lie down either. I had intense vertigo if I even so much as moved my head one degree in any direction. I was attached to a catheter and a pay-TV system that was all Dutch programmes. On top of all this, I couldn't sleep and didn't sleep for four days. There was a clock on the wall opposite me and the hands on that clock were the measure of the most excruciatingly slow passage of time. Sometimes even the second hand would pause. It would just challenge me to blink first before it finally clicked over into the next sixtieth of a minute interval. It was like playing

Grandmother's Footsteps with an actual statue. It would be five past five in the morning and I would close my eyes against a wave of nausea, someone would walk past the room and not come in, I would think of calling out but couldn't. Then I would open my eyes and it was still five past fucking five in the morning.

Oh – now I am enjoying myself and writing bonus, bonus material!

I started a new list. Careers I could have had. Jobs I could have done. Could still do, I don't want to be defeatist.

No.1 – Cinema Programmer (you know, in an arthouse cinema that doesn't just show the latest films).

This is my Nicolas Cage season:

- *Moonstruck* (one of the best films ever!)
- *Color Out Of Space* (recent good one)
- *Face/Off* (with John Travolta!)
- *Leaving Las Vegas* and *Honeymoon In Vegas* double bill
- *The Rock* and *Con Air* (double bill)
- *Peggy Sue Got Married*
- *Mandy*
- *Wild At Heart* (tentpole film in the middle of the season)
- *Bad Lieutenant Port of Call New Orleans*
- *Matchstick Men* (underrated, excellent film)
- *Knowing* (underrated, very good film)
- *Joe* (he is brilliant in this)
- *Vampire's Kiss* (bonus midnight screening. It is unwatchable but you have to have watched it.)

And, of course, I would follow the Nicolas Cage with an Adam Sandler season. I watched *Uncut Gems* again last night. How on earth did Adam Sandler not get an Oscar nomination in whatever year that was? Who are these people that decide these things?

So...

- *Spanglish* (same director as *Terms of Endearment*)
- *Funny People* (excellent)
- *Punch Drunk Love* (just because it's P.T. Anderson, I don't really rate it that much)
- *The Wedding Singer* (you have to have this one)
- *Happy Gilmore* (you have to have this one too)
- *The Meyerowitz Stories* (I would have married him in this)
- *50 First Dates* (second best film he made with Drew Barrymore)
- *Big Daddy* (for the poster alone)
- *Murder Mystery* (best film with Jennifer Aniston)
- *Uncut Gems* (masterpiece)

And that is the end on the book. I promise! Check for yourself – there literally are no more pages!!

P.S. Please watch *The Sixth Sense* – it is marvellous!